A
Harlequin
Romance

OTHER

Harlequin Romances

by MARY BURCHELL

THE GIRL
IN THE BLUE DRESS

by

MARY BURCHELL

HARLEQUIN BOOKS   TORONTO
WINNIPEG

Original hard cover edition published
by Mills & Boon Limited

.

SBN 373-01947-5

Harlequin edition published February 1976

Printed in Canada

CHAPTER ONE

BEVERLEY spread out the "Northern Counties Advertiser" upon the dining-room table and turned the pages quickly until she came to the section headed "Miscellaneous." Then she ran a trembling finger down the distressingly long column until—

"It's in!" she cried. "There it is. They've put it in this week. Oh, dear — rather near the end, I'm afraid. But perhaps some people start reading from the bottom of the column."

"Why should they?" enquired Aunt Ellen, who was inclined to ask questions like that, owing to a pessimistic outlook on life.

"Well — one does sometimes, you know. At least, I know I often do. With the telephone directory, for instance."

"This isn't the telephone directory," said Aunt Ellen. To which objection there was not, of course, any really good reply.

" 'High-class dressmaker and tailoress,' " Beverley read aloud, though she could, in actual fact, have recited the advertisement in her sleep, " 'welcomes work, either in own home or visiting by the day. Original designs. Reasonable terms. Highest references. Apply Box 641.' — You know, I think it sounds really attractive."

"Except that everyone has different ideas on the meaning of 'reasonable terms,' " replied Aunt Ellen gloomily.

"Oh, Aunt Ellen, you're hopeless!" Beverley laughed. "I shall go and show it to Mother. She is always optimistic and cheering."

"That's probably why she is often disappointed." Aunt Ellen shook her head in a disillusioned manner. But Beverley was already in the next room, standing by her mother's bed, smiling down at her.

"It's in, Mother! And it looks fine."

"Let me see, dear." Mrs. Farman — whose spirits had never been really subdued, either by years of crippling arthritis or recent widowhood — took the paper eagerly. "Why, what a good position for the advertisement!"

"Do you think so?" Beverley's dark eyes shone. "But — why, exactly?"

"Because it comes just where anyone would fold the paper. Look — there it is, right at the top of the fold."

"Oh, Mother, you're quite right! You really do have a talent for seeing advantages. Aunt Ellen said — oh, well, never mind."

"No, no, don't worry about Ellen's gloom, bless her heart," Mrs. Farman said cheerfully. "She is pure gold — but in its rather lumpy state. She always expected the worst, even when we were children. I remember once—" she put down the paper and looked reminiscent — "that she even refused to fly her toy balloon in case a bird pecked it. And the odd thing was that when I at last persuaded her to do so, a wretched bird did peck it. Isn't life exasperating?"

Beverley laughed, but she hung over the newspaper again eagerly.

"It was an inspiration of yours that I should offer to go out to people's houses. Hardly anyone will do that nowadays. And yet it's much the best way really. At any rate in a scattered country district like this."

"Of course." Mrs. Farman nodded emphatically. "It was always done when I was a girl. We had a Miss Popplejohn, I remember. She wore high-necked blouses and what used to be called a false front — fuzzy hair looming rather menacingly over the brow, you know — and had very cold hands."

"Oh, Mother—" Beverley looked doubtful — "do you think that's what people still expect? Because if so, I don't fill the bill at all."

"But, darling, think what a lovely surprise you would be if anyone were expecting the Popplejohn pattern. You are a great improvement on her."

"So long as I look sufficiently old and responsible."

Beverley glanced rather anxiously in the mirror opposite, and felt that her wide dark eyes and her fair hair and rather round face did not suggest either age or responsibility.

"Do you think I look twenty-two?" she enquired.

"No. You look about nineteen," replied her mother exactly. "But you also look very nice and capable. I should engage you on the spot, myself."

"But then you're not altogether unprejudiced," laughed Beverley. But she felt immensely cheered.

That was the amazing thing about Mother. Although she had been an invalid for so long, and although things had been very difficult indeed since Father died, less than a year ago, the fact was that she was the recipient of more confidences than anyone else in the village, and an acknowledged tonic for any-one who was feeling depressed.

It was odd that her sister was so very much the reverse. Unless, of course, Aunt Ellen was right in saying that *someone* had to have her feet on the ground. Whatever that tiresomely often-repeated phrase might mean.

Unquestionably, the smooth running of the house-hold owed much to Aunt Ellen, and both Beverley and her mother were gratefully aware of this. Her practical skill, her genuine kindness — somewhat too well concealed beneath a critical exterior — her true devotion to her sister and her sister's child — these were all qualities which might have endeared Aunt Ellen to one. If only a little light-hearted gaiety and hopefulness had gone with all this.

As it was, when the two widowed sisters had joined forces, after the sudden death of Beverley's father the previous year, there was no doubt that the prac-tical advantages were considerable. And so one over-looked some of the more trying aspects of an other-wise convenient arrangement.

Above all, the presence of Aunt Ellen did release Beverley for work which would augment the very modest family resources.

For two years she had worked in London, during

7

her father's lifetime, in one of the top fashion houses, thereby gaining invaluable experience in the profession she was determined to make her own. In her more extravagant moments of phantasy, she saw herself as a great dress designer one day. But, even in her humblest view of the future, she knew, quite objectively, that she was exceptionally gifted, both as a designer and as an actual worker.

She was, as even the head of the London workroom had admitted, by nature a "cutter." Which may sound like a sort of boast to some, but which is, in this connection, an accolade accorded only to those who may be trusted with the styling of a dress or coat, as well as the detailed sewing.

Had her father lived, Beverley would probably have pursued her career through the various stages of the fashion world in town. But recently — knowing how greatly her mother depended on her, both personally and financially — she had decided to try the experiment of living at home and being more or less an independent worker.

She knew she could not hope to make a good living in her own village alone. But her advertisement had been worded with the intention of finding some compromise between coming to a dead end in the village and leaving home altogether — even for Castleton, which was the nearest big town.

During the next few days, Beverley waited eagerly for the first replies — which she imagined being sent on in batches of two or three (possibly even six or eight), every few days.

To her mother she made all sorts of hopeful confidences. But there was one other person with whom she also shared her hopes. And that was Geoffrey Revian.

Not that Geoffrey was overwhelmingly interested. You could hardly expect a real artist to find the ups and downs of a dressmaking venture entirely absorbing. But at least he tended to show an amused and friendly interest in most things which concerned Beverley.

She had known Geoffrey since she was twelve, and loved him since she was twelve and a half. Although he was six or seven years older than she, it had always seemed quite natural for him to confide his hopes and his difficulties to her, and there was little she did not know about the crises of his early twenties, when he had had such a hard struggle to set his feet on the path he was determined to travel.

Beverley knew all about how his father had wanted him to go into his flourishing drapery business in Castleton, and how Geoffrey — who had never wanted to be anything but an artist — had steadfastly refused. Thanks to a very small income left him by his grandmother, he had been able to stick to his resolve. But it had been a bitter struggle, both financially and personally.

In those early days, perhaps he had confided more than he had realized to the dark-eyed child who listened so raptly to him. At any rate, she used to come and watch him at work, on summer evenings after her homework was done. And to her dying day she would be proud of the fact that the first picture he ever exhibited and sold was a portrait of herself, sitting there on the grass, in her very ordinary blue and white cotton dress.

Unfortunately this early success was not followed by very many others. At least, it had not been up to now. But Beverley knew perfectly well that many of the best artists had a terrible struggle at first, and she entirely agreed with Geoffrey that the important thing was to go on believing in oneself, and that one day — one day — success would come.

She believed in him with all her heart and soul. Even during the two years in London, she had continued to write encouragement to him. But she sometimes thought that if she had been Geoffrey, she would have given up the struggle long ago, and gone into the drapery business and been content to paint in her spare time.

But she had a vaguely guilty feeling that this was rather poor-spirited of her.

Meanwhile, Geoffrey lived in a small but picturesque and reasonably comfortable cottage on the outskirts of the village, and was regarded with a mixture of awe and condescension by the village folk, according to whether they regarded painting as an accomplishment or a harmless weakness.

"One of these days, I'll have to do another picture of you," Geoffrey told her, as she sat watching him two or three evenings after the advertisement had come out in the "Advertiser." "You are eminently paintable. I'm not quite sure why, because there's nothing elusive or mysterious about you. Perhaps it's the complete reality of you. And those wide cheekbones, of course. Anyway — I believe you're a sort of mascot for me. I have a feeling I might strike lucky with you again."

"Oh, Geoffrey, how I wish you could!" She thought it was wonderful how he just went on, obstinately determined to impress himself upon an indifferent world one day. "It would be marvellous if you really started to make a living at your work."

"Artistic recognition would be even more marvellous," he said, standing back from his easel to regard what he had just completed.

"Yes, of course," she agreed quickly. "But the other would be useful too. At least, I know that's how I feel about my work. Though of course, that's something very different," she added, in case he should think she imagined dressmaking was on the same level as real art.

"Very different," he agreed, but without rancour. And then — perhaps because he was genuinely interested in her affairs, he asked, "Any replies yet from your advertisement?"

"No. It's a bit — disappointing, isn't it? Or do you think the newspaper people wait until there are several replies, just to make it worth while sending?"

"My guess is that they're trying to find a sack big enough to take all the replies," Geoffrey said good-humouredly. "I only wish I could afford to have you come and make shirts and pyjamas for me."

She thought how she would have loved to do just that. Or, indeed, anything that would link her day-to-day life with Geoffrey. And she wondered, for the hundredth time, if he ever felt at all as she did.

She knew that he considered he was too poor to marry anyone, because he had told her so, years ago, when she was only about sixteen. But that did not prevent her wondering what his reactions would be, if and when he found artistic recognition *and* a good living through his painting.

When she got home, Aunt Ellen greeted her with, "Nothing by the evening post," and somehow she managed to make that sound as though there never would be anything by any post.

But the next morning, patience and optimism were rewarded at last. For when Beverley came downstairs, Jim, the postman, was just coming up the garden path. She saw him through the open front doorway, and rushed to collect from his hand the large envelope, with "Northern Counties Advertiser" stamped on the flap at the back.

Quite a large envelope — but rather thin. Still——

She tore it open eagerly, and one letter fell out. She shook the envelope and peered inside. But — no, there was only one reply. Out of all the people she had imagined reading her advertisement and being favourably impressed by it — only one had thought fit to reply.

It was a sobering thought. But even one reply was better than none. So, trembling with eagerness, Beverley tore open the smaller envelope and drew out a single sheet of good, thick writing paper. The address at the top was sufficiently impressive: "Huntingford Grange, Huntingford, Nr. Castleton."

"Dear Madam," the letter ran, in firm, legible handwriting, "With reference to your advertisement in this week's 'Advertiser,' I should like to discuss with you the possibility of your doing some work for me and my daughters.

"I see you are willing to come out daily to work at the houses of your clients, and this would possibly be the best arrangement here, as we are a little isolated. There would be a pleasant room for you to work in, however, and we have an electric sewing-machine.

"The No. 4 bus from Castleton to Ebury passes within a mile of the house, and on certain days it would be possible to collect you by car from the bus stop. Would you kindly let me know which afternoon in the coming week would suit you for preliminary discussion.

"As my eldest daughter will be getting married in the autumn, there will be a good deal of work to be done, should we come to a mutually satisfactory arrangement. — Yours truly, Viola Wane."

It was businesslike and to the point. It held out promise of a considerable amount of most congenial work. And the cool but courteous terms of the letter suggested to Beverley's mind a likeable employer.

"Mother—" she dashed into her mother's room, where Aunt Ellen was just arranging breakfast on a bedside table — "Mother, there's a perfectly lovely reply to my advertisement! Just listen to this!" And she read the letter aloud, while her mother — and even Aunt Ellen too — listened with the greatest attention.

"Mrs. Wayne — of Huntingford Grange?" Mrs. Farman considered the name. "I've heard of them, of course, but I can't recall much about them. And yet — weren't they mentioned in some connection recently?"

"They don't exactly belong to the district," said Aunt Ellen — meaning that their ancestors were not mentioned in the local equivalent of the Doomsday Book. "The eldest daughter got engaged at the beginning of the year to that man who bought up so much land round Huntingford. You remember — he was *quite* a stranger, with an odd sort of name. Franklin Something. Lyall — Lovell — no. *Lowell.* That was it. Franklin Lowell. They say he's almost a millionaire," she added austerely.

"All the better," declared Beverley briskly. "I'd be delighted to work for a millionaire's future bride.

Anyway, this family ought to have a pretty generous interpretation of the expression 'reasonable terms!'"

"It's the bride's mother you'll be working for," Aunt Ellen reminded her. "And they say the Waynes haven't much money. There are three daughters, I've heard. All as pretty as pictures. But as poor as church mice." She brought out the cliché with a sort of gloomy relish. "You had better make sure of your money before you do too much work. They may not be good payers."

"Have you heard that too?" enquired Beverley, rather tartly.

"No. But it's always best to be cautious when people are having to make a great show on little," Aunt Ellen declared.

"And do they have to make a great show on little?" enquired Mrs. Farman interestedly.

"Well, I suppose so. If the eldest girl is going to marry a millionaire — or near enough — they will be wanting to make as good an appearance as they can. They wouldn't want her to have a wedding to be ashamed of." Aunt Ellen shook her head at the folly of it all.

"And that's why they want me," cried Beverley, looking pink and gratified. "What a lovely assignment to have! I'll see they have a marvellous wedding — at least, so far as the dresses are concerned. Oh, what fun! It's just the sort of thing I'd adore to do. I'll make them look like a Paris dress show — at a fifth of the cost."

"But get your money first," Aunt Ellen warned her.

"Nonsense, Ellen," said Mrs. Farman. "No dressmaker can ask for her money in advance. Whoever heard of such a thing?"

"I meant in advance of the wedding," retorted Aunt Ellen unmoved. "Before they've spent all they have on the champagne and suchlike."

"I shall be perfectly businesslike," Beverley assured her a little loftily. "But I certainly am not going to start by being suspicious or grasping. I shall telephone—" a glance at the notepaper assured her that the impoverished Waynes did at least run to a telephone— "and arrange to go over and discuss things as soon as possible."

"You might even arrange it for this afternoon." Mrs. Farman exchanged a sparkling smile with her eager daughter. "How very fortunate that the No. 4 bus actually goes right through the village."

"It's a poor service, though," Aunt Ellen reminded them both. But neither paid any attention to this. The poorness of the No. 4 bus service had been part of their lives for too long for them to start worrying about that now.

As soon as she had finished her rather hasty breakfast, Beverley went out to the callbox across the road, to telephone to Mrs. Wayne.

It was a sunny morning, and as she stood there in the callbox, she could see all the way down the main street of the village to the pretty little market square at the end. She could even see the red roof of Geoffrey's cottage, and she wondered what *he* would say to this delightful development of her plan.

The local exchange (which consisted of one willing but slightly unofficial young woman) took some time to get the number, and Beverley had leisure to prop her elbow on a pile of out-of-date directories and enjoy the scene.

Like most villages in the north of England, Binwick (pronounced, of course, Binnick — to the satisfaction of the natives and the confusion of visitors) had a sort of sturdy charm. Most of the houses were of stone, and on the whole, the designs were strictly utilitarian. But almost all of them had beautiful gardens in which old-fashioned flowers rioted gloriously.

The village church was a gem of Norman architecture. And if its heating system did seem to hail from some time in the Middle Ages, so did its stained glass, which was very beautiful.

In any case, Beverley knew and loved every corner of the place, and — absorbed though she was in the interest of the moment — she looked upon it with immense satisfaction. Until the voice of the exchange said with encouragement, "I'm putting you through now."

An alarming series of clickings and whirrings then took place. After which a clear, pleasant voice said, "Huntingford two-three. Mrs. Wayne speaking."

Trying to sound very businesslike and experienced, Beverey explained her identity and her willingness to come and see Mrs. Wayne as soon as possible.

"Then what about this afternoon?" asked the pleasant voice. "I'm afraid I shall have to ask you to walk up from the bus-stop — which is the Crown Hotel in Donham. But it is slightly under a mile, and a very pretty walk."

"I don't mind a bit," Beverley assured her. "I'll catch the two o'clock bus from here and should be at the Grange soon after three."

"Very good. We will expect you then," said Mrs. Wayne.

And she rang off, leaving Beverley with the impression that the "we" must include all the daughters. Whereupon she immediately saw herself as the centre of an eager circle of beautiful girls, all waiting to be exquisitely dressed for that most picturesque and touching of all occasions — a wedding.

It was a dressmakers' dream of bliss, Beverley thought, and she ran back home full of happy enthusiasm.

Her mother received the news of the early meeting with gratifying interest, and even Aunt Ellen could find nothing wrong with the plan. So that Beverley set off to do the morning's shopping in a state of happiness which made it difficult for her not to tell her news to everyone she met.

She allowed herself ten minutes from her shopping to call in and tell Geoffrey the news. But, disappointingly, there was no answer to her knock. She knocked again and waited a few minutes. But then she decided that he must have gone away for the day — possibly to Castleton — and she retraced her way home, sorry not to have seen him but reflecting philosophically that she would have even more to tell him when they did meet.

Not since she had set out for London on her first job had she felt such a pleasant thrill of half-nervous excitement and anticipation as assailed her when she boarded the No. 4 bus that afternoon.

To most people, of course, she would merely have been that nice young dressmaker, Beverley Farman, going off to do some work at one of the big houses in the neighbourhood. But to herself she was setting out on a new and untried venture which might yield who knew what interesting experiences?

The drive was an attractive one — most of it over high ground from which one had fine views across woodland and farmland, right away to where the cold North Sea sketched a grey-blue line along the horizon.

It was ten minutes to three when the bus set her down at the Crown. And, just as Beverley was looking round, to see whom she could ask for directions to Huntingford Grange, a young man got out of a car parked on the other side of the street and came across to her.

"Are you Miss Farman?" he enquired, in a pleasant voice which immediately reminded her of the voice on the telephone that morning.

"Yes, I am." Beverley smiled expectantly at him.

"I thought you must be, since you were the only person who got off. But you look a bit like your own niece, somehow. Mother told me you would be elderly and precise. Will you come across the road? I have the car here and will drive you up home."

"Thank you." Beverley accompanied him across the street. "But — do tell me — what made you think I would be elderly and precise?"

"Well, my mother said you would be. They used to have someone come and do sewing in their family when she was a girl. Her name was Miss Popplejohn and——"

"Not *really?*" Beverley was enchanted. "She used to do sewing for my mother too. There simply couldn't be two of them with a name like that, could there?"

The young man said quite impossible, and did Beverley's Miss Popplejohn wear high necks and have fuzzy hair?

"Yes, she did. It wasn't her own, though. The bit at the front, I mean. And Mother said she had very cold hands."

By now, with the intimate link of Miss Popplejohn, they felt quite old friends, and as they got into the car, he said,

"I didn't introduce myself. I'm Andrew Wayne."

"I gathered that you must be. At least, that you must be a young Mr. Wayne. Are you the only one?"

"I'm the only son, if that's what you mean. I have three sisters, though."

"Yes, I've heard of them. They are all very beautiful, aren't they?"

"We-ell, I don't know about that." Andrew Wayne considered the statement with the critical air of one who found other people's sisters more beautiful. "I suppose they are a pretty good-looking bunch. Sara certainly is. She's the eldest and is getting married in the autumn. She's twenty-two. Three years younger than I am," he added gratuitously.

"And the others?" enquired Beverley, with that inoffensive but genuine interest which is always flatteringly pleasant.

"Madeleine is a couple of years younger than Sara——"

"She'll be a bridesmaid, of course?" interrupted Beverley, whose mind was already on the wedding procession.

"I suppose so. Yes — of course she will. And Toni — her real name's Antoinette — will be train-bearer or something. Though how anyone's going to guarantee that she won't step on the train I don't know. She has a talent, amounting almost to genius, for doing and saying the very thing you hoped she wouldn't."

Beverley laughed and asked how old Toni was.

"She's twelve — which of course means a very big gap between her and the rest of us. I guess we spoil her in some ways, and then we often forget she is really a child. Which means that she's a mixture of disconcerting knowledge and almost equally disconcerting innocence." But Toni's brother grinned as he said this, with an air of reminiscent indulgence, and Beverley rather thought that he had a special liking for his youngest sister.

Before she could ask any more, or he could impart further information, they arrived at Huntingford Grange, which turned out to be a somewhat imposing eighteenth-century house, with nothing specially to commend it, beyond its size, its solidity and its very beautiful position on top of a hill.

From the drive in front of the house — and Beverley turned to look around her — it was possible to see over miles of countryside, again to the dark rim of the cold North Sea. And although it was a warm day in May, a fresh breeze blew up here, bending the flowering bushes which grew in the shrubbery on either side of the house.

"Come on in, and I'll find someone for you." Andrew ran up the half-dozen steps to the front door, and Beverley followed him.

As she did so, she thought, quite impersonally, what a well-set-up young man he was, and that — with his dark hair and very blue eyes — he was not at all unworthy to be the brother of three beautiful sisters.

At his cheerful, but informal shout of "Mother!" a tall, good-looking woman in her late forties or early fifties came out of a room at the end of the hall. She was so like him that there would have been no doubting the relationship, even without this informal identification.

"Here is Miss Farman, Mother," Andrew Wayne explained. "She's about thirty-five years younger than you expected. But she knows all about Miss Popplejohn, because Miss P. used to work for *her* mother too."

"Really?" Mrs. Wayne smiled and shook hands with Beverley. But although there was a glint of

18

genuine amusement in her very blue eyes, there was also a slight air of reserve about her which did not invite the same gay camaraderie as her son seemed to enjoy. Beverley, however, did not like her any the less for that.

"Your mother must have lived on the other side of the county when she was a girl, then," she said.

"Yes, she did. Her name was Trenton then. Angela Trenton," Beverley explained. "My grandfather was the Vicar of St. Stephen-in-the-Woods."

"Is that so?" Mrs. Wayne looked courteously interested, but not as though she wished to pursue the subject of Beverley's antecedents. "Would you like to come this way, and I will show you the sewing-room, and we can have a talk."

She led the way upstairs. Up two flights of stairs, in fact. To a large, light room which she explained had once been the children's schoolroom. Here there was, Beverley noted in a quick, comprehensive glance round, almost everything that a good dressmaker could require.

A large table for cutting, an adjustable model, and an electric sewing-machine standing in an excellent light from two windows.

A small fire burned in the grate, and as the room stood high and had several windows in it, this was by no means unwelcome, in spite of the brightness of the day. If she were going to spend much of the next few weeks — possibly even months — working here, she would not have much to complain of, Beverley thought.

At Mrs. Wayne's invitation, she sat down in a chair near the fire, opposite her proposed employer, and waited to hear what the older woman had to say.

"Did you make the dress and coat you are wearing?" was Mrs. Wayne's first enquiry.

"Yes." Beverley glanced down at her light-weight grey coat and matching dress, with the unusual wide white collar.

"It's charming. So very simple and yet stylish. Was it your own design and cut?"

19

"Oh, yes. At least, this particular dress was an adaptation from something I liked but which was a trifle too old for me," Beverley explained.

"I see. And that kind of adaptation holds no difficulties for you?"

"No. I don't think so. I like making my own designs entirely too. But good ideas can always be adapted to individual needs and tastes."

Mrs. Wayne nodded and seemed satisfied. Then she went into the question of business arrangements, and Beverley noted — with a mixture of amusement and anxiety — that her ideas of "reasonable terms" tended more towards Aunt Ellen's pessimistic prophecies than her own high hopes.

"Your terms are rather high, Miss Farman," Mrs. Wayne said frankly.

"My work is very good, Mrs. Wayne," Beverley replied, equally frankly. "If you went to any good London fashion house you would pay very much more."

"And your work is equal to that?" Mrs. Wayne did not sound exactly sceptical, but as though she needed to be convinced.

"I think so. But the only way to make sure would be for you to try me out on one or two things. If you genuinely felt the work was not worth what I am asking, I would not refuse to discuss our arrangement again."

"Hm, that is fair enough," Mrs. Wayne conceded. "Then I think the best thing would be for you to start on — let us say — a couple of informal dresses for my eldest daughter, who is getting married in the autumn, as I told you, and needs a good many things for her trousseau, of course."

"I should like to do that," Beverley began. But before they could take the discussion further the door opened, and a small, dark-haired girl who was undoubtedly Toni came in.

"Oh, Mother, is this Miss Farman who's going to make dresses for us all?" she demanded with interest. "And can she make a party dress for me, the *very first* thing? Because it's Wendy Tulley's birthday party next month, and I simply haven't got *anything*. Not anything at all."

"No, Toni——"

"Oh, Mother!" The stricken wail betokened agony of mind, but the interested glance in Beverley's direction suggested that the misery was only skin deep.

"Don't make that ridiculous noise," said her mother without passion. "And go down and ask Sara to come up here, there's a good child."

"May I come up too? I *love* to hear clothes discussed."

"Very well. But be quick."

Toni whisked off immediately and Mrs. Wayne smiled at Beverley.

"She isn't as pretty as the other two," she said objectively. "But she is just beginning to get clothes-conscious."

"She is very attractive looking and would be fun to dress," Beverley replied sincerely. "I hope you are going to let her have her party frock. Clothes for children of that age *are* rather fun."

"Well — we'll see. There is no lack of material, anyway." And, to Beverley's astonishment, Mrs. Wayne went over to a huge, old-fashioned press, which stood in the corner of the room, and, opening it, displayed twenty or more parcels which obviously contained material. Some of them were completely shrouded in wrapping paper, but some of the parcels were open at the end, so that one caught glimpses of quite lovely silks and cottons of a most exquisite colouring and variety.

"Why——" Beverley drew near, in curiosity and admiration — "what a treasure-house!"

"Yes, they are lovely, aren't they? I have an uncle who is an importer of oriental silks and materials," Mrs. Wayne explained. "He has often given us odd lengths over the years. That's why it seemed so much more sensible to find someone to make these up, rather than spend money on other things."

"I should think so, indeed!" said Beverley, fascinated by the prospect of working in these beautiful materials.

Then Toni came back and with her came quite the loveliest girl Beverley had ever set eyes upon.

Sara Wayne was tall, like her mother and her brother, and she was almost perfectly proportioned — the set and length of her neck being so particularly beautiful that when she turned her lovely head from side to side one could hardly keep one's eyes from her.

Unlike her brother she had brilliantly fair, almost corn-coloured hair, but her eyes were the same intense blue. And the features which in him — and to a certain extent in her mother — were strong and well-defined, were in her exquisitely delicate, and moulded as though by the hand of an artistic genius.

She smiled slightly at Beverley as they were introduced — a sweet, coolly friendly smile. But then her long, unexpectedly dark lashes came down and shadowed her eyes, so that her lovely face took on a secret, faintly mysterious look which must, Beverley thought, be absolutely irresistible to some types of men.

She listened with attention to what her mother and Beverley had to say about the suggested dresses, and she had some good ideas of her own. She smiled occasionally, and when she expressed an opinion, in that cool, pretty voice of hers, it was obvious that she had good taste and knew what suited her.

And yet Beverley had the most extraordinary impression that she was not really interested. She might have been discussing someone else's trousseau, or else arranging for dresses which she herself would wear in a pleasant but unreal masquerade.

"Perhaps it's just her manner," Beverley thought. "She may be very reserved — or shy. And yet — doesn't *any* girl get excited about her trousseau? I know if I were only discussing cotton frocks for a honeymoon with Geoffrey——"

But she quickly jerked her thoughts back from

that path. For, really, whatever hopes she might have about some vague future with Geoffrey had nothing to do with the matter in hand.

Towards the end of the discussion, the third sister, Madeleine, came in, and in some ways Beverley thought her the most attractive of the three. She was not so strictly beautiful as Sara, but much gayer and more animated, and she had the most charming, infectious laugh, which seemed to release a sort of sunny vitality into the room.

Her hair was two or three shades darker than the corn-gold of Sara's, but it curled delightfully round her prettily shaped head, and like all the rest of the family, she had intensely blue, beautifully set eyes.

"I can't imagine anything more exciting than making clothes for such beautiful girls," Beverley said frankly. "I do hope I shall be able to please you all with my work."

"Why, how sweet of you," Madeleine exclaimed, while her elder sister smiled and said nothing.

"I'm sure you'll please me," Toni told her. "Especially if you'll make me a party dress to wear at Wendy Tulley's party. It's next month and I've absolutely nothing——"

"All right, Toni. We'll discuss that later," interrupted her mother. "When could you start work, Miss Farman?"

"As soon as you like."

"Tomorrow?"

"Yes. Tomorrow would be excellent. There is a bus from Binwick soon after half-past eight. I could be here before ten, if that would suit you."

"Would you be available, Sara?" Her mother turned to her.

"Yes, of course," Sara said. And again Beverley had the queer impression that she was not really interested, and also that she had all the time in the world hanging on her beautiful hands.

"Well, that's fine." Mrs. Wayne stood up, with an air of decision. "Toni, will you take Miss Farman downstairs to the little drawing-room, and I'll have

23

some tea sent in. If you'll excuse me, Miss Farman, I have to put through a couple of telephone calls."

Toni seemed very pleased to have social care of the visitor for a short while, and waited rather impatiently while the other two girls said a pleasant goodbye. Then she conducted Beverley downstairs again to a charming room which looked over a fine, but rather neglected garden.

Beverley was secretly somewhat surprised to be treated so much more as a visitor than an employee. But she guessed that this might be a rather special occasion — due possibly to the connection with Miss Popplejohn and the fact that her grandfather had been Vicar of St. Stephen-in-the-Woods. No doubt when she was actually working at the house, her meals would be brought to her on a tray in the schoolroom.

"Do you like going out and sewing for people?" Toni enquired, hopping up and down on one foot and regarding Beverley with interest.

"I think I shall like coming out and sewing for you," Beverley told her, not choosing to say that this was the first time she had done such a thing. "It's always fun doing clothes for a wedding."

"Is it? Why?"

"Oh, well — there is something so romantic and picturesque about a wedding, I suppose. And one tries to have everything just as beautiful as it can be, for such an occasion. Your sister will make a lovely bride."

"Ye-es. She's going to marry Franklin Lowell, you know. Have you heard of him?" Toni enquired.

"Just his name."

"He's very rich."

"Is he?" said Beverley, a little uncomfortably.

"Yes. That's him — over there." Toni pointed to a photograph which stood on top of a bureau near the window, and Beverley — thinking to keep this conversation from becoming any more personal — went over to examine it.

The photograph was of a man in shirt and riding

24

breeches, and Beverley immediately had the most overwhelming impression of someone tall and strong and with immense vitality. He was looking straight out of the photograph and smiling slightly, in a not entirely reassuring manner.

"He looks — quite a personality," Beverley said as non-committally as possible. But she immediately had Toni at her elbow, ready to continue the subject.

"Do you think so? Would *you* like to marry him?"

"Well—" Beverley was rather startled by the unexpected question, posed in a perfectly serious manner — "I can't say he's my type, exactly. But——"

"If you promise not to tell anyone, I'll tell you a *deadly* secret," Toni interrupted, in a mysterious but entirely friendly manner.

"But I don't want to hear any deadly secrets," Beverley began firmly.

Toni, however, didn't seem to pay much attention to that. The secret had just suddenly got too big for her and she was going to tell it or burst.

"It's about Sara," she said. "Franklin isn't *her* type either. She doesn't want to marry him a bit."

"You mustn't tell me such things! It isn't my business and it isn't your business either," Beverley exclaimed sharply.

"But I have to tell someone because I'm *worried.*" And suddenly big tears stood in Toni's bright eyes. "I can't tell anyone in the family, because they all want her to marry Franklin who's so rich. But she really wants to marry quite a poor man. He's an artist, and his name's Geoffrey Revian."

CHAPTER TWO

FOR PERHAPS two seconds Beverley stared at the little girl in appalled silence. Then — now entirely unheeding of the fact that one simply did not encourage a child to discuss other people's private affairs — she said, a trifle hoarsely,

"Di-did you say — Geoffrey Revian?"

"Yes." Toni nodded emphatically. "He painted a portrait of Sara, and she got fond of him and——"

"But how do you *know?* I mean — oh, we shouldn't be talking about this at all. It — it isn't our business," stammered Beverley distractedly, as her natural sense of integrity returned to her. "You mustn't tell me your sister's private affairs. I am a stranger and——"

"That's why I told you," Toni explained simply.

"But there's nothing I can do about it! Even if it concerned me. Which it does not," Beverley said quickly. And then, for a bitter moment, she thought of Geoffrey, and how deeply this really did concern her.

"No. I don't expect there's anything that *anyone* can do about it," agreed Toni mournfully. "I expect Sara will just marry Franklin and gradually die of a broken heart."

"Nonsense. No one does that in real life," Beverley asserted, as reassuringly as she could. Though the almost physical ache which she seemed to feel in the region of her own heart made her wonder if this were quite true.

"Anyway, I feel better now I've told you." Toni seemed immensely relieved and cheered suddenly. Almost as though she had literally shifted her dreadful burden to Beverley.

"Well, I'm glad of that." Beverley spoke almost absently. "But—" wrong though it was, she knew, to continue the subject, there was one question she simply had to ask — "how can you possibly be sure that you have this right? You may have made some mistake, you know. Your sister might have liked the — the other man once, but decided later that she wanted to marry Mr. Lowell. Lots of girls do that."

She was even slightly cheered herself by the presentation of this theory. But Toni shook her dark head determinedly.

"Not Sara."

"But you can't be sure!"

"Yes, I can." Toni seemed rather affronted at having her version of the story called in question. "She knew him quite a while before Franklin came along——"

"While I was away in London!" thought Beverley with a pang.

"—And then, after she got engaged, Franklin wanted a portrait of her for his house, and he said he knew a good artist in the district, and it turned out to be this Geoffrey Revian. — What did you say?"

"Nothing," said Beverley helplessly, unable now even to attempt to stop this flood of chilling information.

"Well, he used to come here to paint her, and they got more friendly still, I guess. And one day I went in and he had his arms round her and she was crying and——"

"Don't tell me any more! I won't *hear* any more," cried Beverley angrily. "If you must tell someone, you had better tell your mother — or your other sister. It's more their affair than mine."

"But I couldn't tell them," Toni explained patiently. "They all want Sara to marry Franklin, because then there won't have to be a mortgage on the house and all the bills will get paid, and Madeleine will have a season in London. And so shall I, I suppose, when the time comes," she added reflectively. "Though *I* would rather do without the season and have Sara marry whoever she really wants."

This was so palpably true, in a naïve way, that Beverley felt her heart warm to the little girl, in spite of the fact that she seemed to have a terrifying talent for acquiring information which she was supposed not to know.

"Well, perhaps——" Beverley sighed, but felt she must offer some form of comfort to the child — "perhaps everything will work out all right, in the end. It's surprising how often one worries about things that never happen."

"You mean——" Toni looked hopeful — "that Sara may never marry Franklin, after all? — that even now she might marry this Geoffrey Revian instead?"

"No!" Beverley spoke sharply, because this suggestion hurt quite unbearably. "I meant that she may well find she is fond of — of her fiancé, and that in actual fact he is the man she wants, after all."

Toni looked at Beverley in unconvinced silence for a moment. Then she said reflectively,

"You haven't seen Franklin yet, have you?"

"N-no." Beverley was oddly impressed by the tone. "But the photograph doesn't suggest that he is a — an unpleasant person in any way."

"Oh, no. Not unpleasant," Toni conceded. "In fact, he is rather nice, and very generous. But he is kind of — overwhelming. There isn't much room for anyone else when he is around."

In spite of herself, Beverley glanced at the photograph once more, and she could not help thinking that, for a little girl, Toni had a good deal of natural judgment.

Then — to her mingled relief and disappointment — footsteps were heard in the passage, and their agitating tête-à-tête was obviously at an end. A moment later tea was brought in by a maid, and almost immediately afterwards Mrs. Wayne rejoined them.

"I hope Toni has managed to entertain you." Mrs. Wayne smiled at her youngest child, with an indulgence Beverley felt she would hardly have displayed if she could have known just what form Toni's entertainment had taken.

But Beverley said politely, "Yes, indeed." And

then they had tea, and it was obvious that the social part of this visit was over.

"I am afraid you will have to walk down to the bus stop," Mrs. Wayne said. "My son has taken the car off somewhere. It was just a chance that he was available earlier this afternoon. I hope you don't mind."

"Not in the least," Beverley assured her. "I expected to walk both ways, and it's a pleasant walk."

"Well — it gets a little wearisome if you have to do it too often." Mrs. Wayne smiled. "But whenever it is possible to arrange a lift for you I will do so, and perhaps you won't mind the other times too much."

Once more Beverley gave an assurance that she would not. And, after repeating that she would be back, ready to start work, before ten o'clock next morning, she took her leave. Toni, with obvious friendliness, accompanied her to the front door, and, looking at the big hall clock, said,

"You'll have to hurry, Miss Farman. The bus goes from the Crown at a quarter past five, I think."

Spurred on by this thought, Beverley actually ran part of the way along the lane, for she knew there would probably be a wait of nearly two hours between buses. The hurrying kept her from thinking too deeply about her afternoon visit. But nothing could entirely hold at bay the anxious thoughts which Toni's revelation had prompted.

She tried to tell herself, as she half walked, half ran along, that the really important event of the afternoon was the securing of a large order for most congenial and interesting work. But, in the back of her mind, looming over every other consideration, was the revelation which the youngest Wayne daughter had insisted on making to her.

"She is only a child," Beverley told herself. "She has overheard some half-truths and seen one or two things which she has misinterpreted. Then she put all of them together and has distressed herself badly with her own garbled version of the situation. That's what it is."

But she did not really believe this. She believed that what Toni had told her was substantially the truth. Somehow, in a naïve, disconnected way, the story had the ring of truth about it. And, if that were the case — what of her own position with regard to Geoffrey?

Until that moment, somehow, Beverley had never really thought of anyone supplanting herself in Geoffrey's affections. She had accepted the fact that it might be years before he felt in a position to marry *her* — if ever. But that he would want to marry someone else had not entered her calculations. She had always thought of him as someone who would not think seriously about any girl.

Now she saw how ridiculous and untenable such a theory must be. Like everyone else in the world, Geoffrey might have his firm intentions and make his plans. But, human nature being what it is, no amount of planning will safeguard one against the sudden capitulation of the heart.

Why should he not fall in love with Sara Wayne? She was lovely enough, in all conscience.

And, as she reached this point in her thoughts, Beverley slackened her pace. She forgot about the bus, and thought only of the unspeakable desert which life would become if she had to face the fact that Geoffrey belonged to someone else, so far as his affections were concerned.

It was not as though she could ask him anything about it. For one thing, if he did not choose to confide in her — and why should he? — it was not for her to force the issue. And, in any case, she had no right to the information in the first place.

She even wondered remorsefully now if she should somehow have managed to stop Toni before she had said so much. But it was no good going back over that ground now.

And then Beverley turned the last curve in the lane, and was immediately presented with a practical fact which drove melancholy reflections from her mind for the moment. The bus-stop was in full view, though a good hundred yards away. And there, just drawing up to decant a couple of passengers and take up two or three more, was her bus.

Too late she broke into the sharpest sprint she could manage. She had not covered half the intervening distance before the bus moved off once more. And Beverley was left panting and waving fruitlessly, while the bus sailed away over the hill into the distance.

It was the most maddening thing! For something like two hours she would have to sit there on a bench — at least there was a bench! — kicking her heels and waiting for the next bus.

She could hardly go back to the house. She did not know the family well enough for that. And there was a four- or five-mile walk between her and any other bus route that would get her home.

More slowly, since speed did not matter now, she made her way to the bus-stop and stood disconsolately studying the out-of-date and rather fly-blown time-table pasted on the board.

This told her quite a lot about the buses which would not be running on Christmas Day and Bank Holidays, and even stated the times of buses during the winter months. But there was no information about summer services, and she turned away, with a gesture of impatience and disgust.

As she did so a car drove up and a voice called out,

"Have you just missed your bus?"

"Yes, I'm afraid so." She approached the car eagerly.

"Where do you want to go?" The man in the driving-seat leaned over and opened the nearside door.

"Binwick. — Or wherever I can pick up a bus that goes there."

"All right. Jump in. I'm going through there. I'll take you along."

"Oh, *thank* you! But if you could just manage to

overtake the bus and put me down at a stop further on that would do," Beverley assured him, as she climbed into the seat beside the driver.

"Sorry. I shan't be following the bus route. I have to cut across by Steeplemere."

"Well, if you don't mind taking me all the way, that's better still, of course. I'll be home sooner than the bus would take me," Beverley said. And, having slammed the car door, she turned to have a better look at her companion.

She then saw that it was Franklin Lowell.

He was quite unmistakable. The photograph back there in the little drawing-room at Huntingford Grange was really very good of him. Except that it had not conveyed in full measure the almost dynamic impression of energy and vitality which flowed from this big, dark man, with the abrupt but not unfriendly voice.

For a moment Beverley sat wordless, watching his strong, well-shaped hands on the wheel of the car, and wondering what she should say to him.

However, he made it quite easy for her by asking if she belonged to the district.

"Not immediately round here," Beverley explained. "My home is in Binwick. I came here to see Mrs. Wayne. I am going to do some dressmaking for her in the coming weeks." She thought she had better make her position clear at once.

"Is that so?" He sounded quite interested. "I know the Waynes well. In fact, I'm engaged to Sara, the eldest daughter."

"Yes — I know," Beverley said a little shyly.

He flashed her an amused glance.

"How do you know?"

"There is a photograph of you in one of the rooms at the Grange, and the little girl — Toni — was anxious to explain about you."

"She would be." But he sounded good-humoured about it. "She is the most chatty kid I know. Where she acquires all the information she passes on is a mystery to me."

"Yes, indeed," said Beverley with some feeling. Perhaps with more feeling than she knew, for he gave her that bright, half-amused glance again.

"She gave you the family history, I take it?"

"Well—" Beverley smiled with determined composure — "I was glad when her mother came in and cut short any further confidences. It is rather embarrassing to be handed out personal details when you hardly know people."

He laughed.

"Don't pay too much attention to what she says. She also has a lively imagination."

"Do you think so?" Beverley simply could not hide her eagerness to have that confirmed.

"Why, of course." He looked slightly surprised. "Don't most children of that age? And Toni has more imagination than most. Did she tell you something that — embarrassed you?"

"Not — exactly."

"I suppose she said that Sara was marrying me for my money, and that, otherwise, the family would be in the workhouse — or whatever the modern equivalent is."

"Oh — not quite." She was a good deal startled at the almost brutally careless candour with which he said that. And yet, after a moment, she was extraordinarily reassured too. For even this uncompromising man would hardly put such an idea into words, if it were even remotely near the unfortunate truth.

"I didn't really pay much attention, you know." She found suddenly that she could laugh quite naturally, because her heart felt immensely lightened of its load. "As you say, all children romance a bit. And the odd thing is that they more than half believe it themselves."

"That goes for a surprising number of grown-ups too," he replied dryly. And then he changed the subject by asking if she had lived long in Binwick.

"All my life," Beverley told him, with a smile. "It's a charming place. Do you know it?"

"Fairly well. I know a very clever artist chap who lives there. I expect you'll know him too."

"You mean Geoffrey Revian."

"Yes. Do you know him?"

"Very well."

"I got him to do a protrait of Sara quite recently. It was very successful."

"I — I'm sure it was."

"The odd thing was that I didn't even know he lived in the district until then. But I'd always been interested in his work. Not that I know much about art. But I bought a picture of his at an exhibition some years ago."

"*Did* you?" She could not help being interested. "What made you buy it? — I mean — if you're not interested in painting."

"I hardly know myself." He laughed slightly, as though he were surprised to find he could not explain any impulse of his own. "It was just a picture of a most charming child, sitting on the grass in a blue and white frock. I suppose she would be about Toni's age. — No, maybe rather more. Say fourteen."

"Not — really?" Beverley laughed slightly in her turn, on a note of incredulous surprise and pleasure. "Was it the — the painting or the subject that made you buy the picture?"

"Both, I suppose. At least, I thought the artist had very cleverly caught the personality of the subject. I remember everything else in the exhibition bored me. But I thought — I'd like to know that girl. She's the kind of kid one would like to have around."

"So you bought it?"

"Yes, I bought it."

"And you still have it?"

"Yes, of course. I don't know that it's of any special value, in the market sense. But I wouldn't part with it for a really fancy price. There's something very sane and lovable about my little girl in the blue and white dress, and although my worst enemy wouldn't call me a fanciful chap, I regard her as a very pleasant companion in my house."

"I'm so glad," Beverley said, and laughed.

"You sound as though you really mean that."

"Well, I do! Have you never thought that your little girl in the blue and white dress must be quite grown up now?"

"Yes, certainly. Why do you say that?"

"Because — though I find it rather embarrassing to tell you so, after all the nice things you have said — I was the little girl in the blue and white dress. It was the first picture Geoffrey ever sold."

"You don't say!" He actually drew the car to a standstill by the roadside and turned to look at her, his eyes alight with interest, and his whole attention so completely fixed on her that she flushed slightly under his scrutiny.

"Tell me what your name is."

"Miss Farman."

"No. Your first name," he said, rather peremptorily. "My little girl in the blue and white dress wouldn't answer to the name of Miss Farman."

"My first name is Beverley."

"Beverley—" he repeated it experimentally — "it's a nice name. And it suits her. You, I mean." Again that bright, penetrating glance travelled over her. "I can see now, of course, that you are exactly as she would have grown up."

"Oh — thank you." She laughed, and once more she felt herself flush. "That's very nice of you — though a trifle embarrassing."

"It need not be. I don't think it's in the least embarrassing. I find it most intriguing," he said. "Like meeting an old friend."

She hardly knew how to take such frankness, and yet she could not be anything but touched and flattered by it.

"You know," she said, "you are a most surprising person. No one would suppose from your general air that you were at all romantic or——"

"I am not in the least," he assured her.

"But you must be," she told him. "No entirely practical and common-sense person would make a

35

friend of a picture and take such obvious pleasure in tracing up the original years later."

"You mean you think it's rather silly of me." He considered that frowningly.

"Indeed I don't! I think it's extraordinarily nice of you. I don't remember when I've felt more gratified. Certainly not since the picture was painted and exhibited. And sold," she added, with a half-wistful smile. For she suddenly remembered with poignant clarity how jubilant Geoffrey and she had been over that first sale.

"Well—" he looked amused again — "that seems to establish this as a very satisfactory meeting on both sides."

And then he drove on once more, while Beverley sat there thinking what an extraordinary day of discoveries this had been.

First there had been the contact with the Waynes, and the work which was going to follow as a consequence. Then there was the revelation which Toni had insisted on forcing upon her. Though this, Beverley was daring to begin to think, was greatly exaggerated and by no means to be taken as seriously as she had at first supposed. And now there was the surprising discovery that Franklin Lowell not only owned the picture of herself as a child, but put a most flatteringly high value on it.

"I should like to see it again," she said on impulse.

"What? — The picture of yourself?"

"Yes."

"Well, you shall. I'll drive you over to my place one of these days, and you shall see how you looked when you were a little girl."

"Thank you," Beverley said. But she wondered a little uncomfortaly if she should have invited that suggestion, and whether the Waynes were the kind of people who drew a very clear social distinction between wealthy fiancés and girls who came to the house to do dressmaking for the family.

During the rest of the drive they talked of unimportant things. But he insisted on taking her right to her own front door, and waved away her thanks when she very earnestly expressed these.

Beverley was aware, from the odd twitching of the front-room curtains, that Aunt ￼ing the scene — no doubt with intense and rather disapproving curiosity. But she managed to say a composed goodbye to Franklin Lowell, and even to give him an impersonal but friendly little wave as he drove away.

Then she went into the house, and immediately Aunt Ellen popped out from the front room to demand,

"For goodness' sake, who was that in the handsome car?"

"That was Franklin Lowell," said Beverley, taking off her hat and running her fingers through her hair, while she tried to look as though it were nothing in her young life to be driven up to the house by a reputed millionaire. Or near enough.

"Franklin Lowell?" Aunt Ellen sounded more scandalized than approving. "But he's engaged to the eldest Wayne girl, surely. You shouldn't go driving around the country with another girl's fiancé!"

"Oh, Aunt Ellen, don't be so stuffy," said Beverley — thereby causing her aunt to look very much offended. "He only gave me a lift home because I missed my bus. But come into Mother's room and hear all about it. I've had the most exciting afternoon!"

Curiosity getting the better of any huffiness, Aunt Ellen followed Beverley into her mother's room. And here — over another cup of tea — Beverley gave a lively account of her first visit to Huntingford Grange.

She missed out all that Toni had said, of course, and she did not give any of her own impressions of Sara's curious listlessness or apparent lack of interest in her trousseau. But she enlarged on the attractive prospects of the actual work, and also on the friendliness which had been shown her.

"Darling, how kind Mrs. Wayne sounds," exclaimed her mother. "She really need not have kept you to tea like that. Or, at least, not in her own drawing-room."

"It's always a mistake to start by being too friendly," observed Aunt Ellen gloomily.

"Why?" enquired her sister flatly.

For a moment Aunt Ellen was nonplussed. Then she expressed it as her opinion that people who started that way usually ended by thinking you were presuming on their friendliness.

"Beverley would *never* presume on anyone," stated Mrs. Farman firmly. "How did you get home, dear? You're too early to have come by the bus, surely?"

Beverley explained about missing the bus and about being given a lift by Franklin Lowell.

"And — just imagine, Mother! — it was Mr. Lowell who bought that picture which Geoffrey painted of me when I was fourteen."

This information so delighted her mother — and even impressed Aunt Ellen — that Beverley had to explain about this too, in detail. And at the end her mother said,

"Fancy Geoffrey never mentioning the fact to you!"

"But he probably didn't know of Mr. Lowell as anything but a name until quite recently."

"He could have told you recently, though," put in Aunt Ellen, in a vaguely censorious tone.

"Oh, I daresay he didn't think of it. Or he didn't think of my ever having any connection with Mr. Lowell or being interested. But I think I shall run down a bit later and see if Geoffrey is in." Carelessly she proposed the one thing she had been longing to do ever since Toni had dealt her that blow. "He will be interested to hear of my meeting with Mr. Lowell."

To her mother — and even to Aunt Ellen — this seemed a perfectly normal procedure. So Beverley spent an hour putting everything in order for her first day's work on the morrow — washing a pair of white gloves, tacking a fresh collar on to her dark working-dress and so on. And then, telling her mother that she would be back in good time for supper, she went off down the village street towards Geoffrey's cottage.

She had very little idea, even now, what she was going to say to him. And certainly she had no intention whatever of asking any leading questions, or in any way showing that she knew of a connection between him and Sara Wayne.

But surely, in the natural course of her account of the day, he would say *something* which would give her a hint of his real position in this story.

After her talk with Franklin Lowell, and the carelessly reassuring things he had said about Toni's lively imagination, she was inclined to take a much more hopeful view of things. She imagined his saying casually,—

"Oh, I know Sara Wayne quite well. I painted her portrait. Lovely girl she is, too. I'd have fallen in love with her myself, if I could have allowed myself the luxury. But, as it is, she's marrying a very nice chap who can well afford to give her the setting she needs."

Oh, if only he would say just that! And in a tone that meant he didn't care about her at all — except as a pretty girl whom he naturally admired.

But, even if he did say that — or something like it — would she entirely believe him? Or would she wonder if he were putting up an elaborate smokescreen, so that she should have no inkling of what was really in his mind and heart?

To imagine that it could have come to that! Her even supposing for one moment that there should be a barrier of deception between her and Geoffrey. She told herself that she should be ashamed to be thinking such a thing, on the strength of no more solid evidence than the chatter of a highly imaginative child.

And, a good deal cheered by her own vehemence, she turned in at the gate of Geoffrey's cottage.

But this time too there was no answer to her knock. And, although she thought it doubtful that he would still be working in his studio at the end of the garden, she went round the house and along the rather untidy path which led to the small converted barn used by Geoffrey as a studio.

As she did so, the most extraordinary sense of misgiving assailed her. It was nothing to do with anything she saw or heard or could in any way account for. Only, as she neared the studio, it seemed to her that her heart sank unaccountably, and she even found that she was trembling.

She paused for a moment by the big old rambler which sprawled in picturesque untidiness over an archway half-way down the path. And, as she did so, the door of the studio opened suddenly — as though someone on the other side of it had wrenched it open.

For a second a girl stood silhouetted in the doorway. Then she banged the door behind her and came running up the path.

There was no time to conceal oneself. Hardly even time to step aside out of her immediate path. In a matter of moments the girl had cleared the distance between them, and, with a great gasp, came to a stop only a yard or two from Beverley.

Beverley caught her breath in a gasp too. For the girl who had run from Geoffrey's studio in such agitation, and now stood staring at her utterly nonplussed, was Sara Wayne.

CHAPTER THREE

"WHATEVER made me think she was listless or indifferent?" was Beverley's first reflection, as she looked back at the lovely, flushed and quivering features of the eldest Wayne girl. And then — "What on earth am I going to say to her?"

It seemed to her that there was at least a whole minute's silence between them. But of course there was nothing of the sort. A minute is a long time, measured out in embarrassed seconds. And there is no sharper inducement to break a silence than the knowledge that someone's self-respect is toppling.

In what seemed to her a somewhat artificial tone, Beverley heard herself say.

"Why, how extraordinary to meet you twice in one day! I suppose you have been to see my friend, Geoffrey Revian, about your portrait?"

"My — my portrait?" stammered Sara. And then she too made an immense effort to recover herself. "Oh — no. That's finished, you know, and — and hanging in Franklin's study. I came——" She groped for words, and Beverley actually found herself wishing pitifully that she could supply her with a good excuse.

Then Sara rallied herself determinedly and said, almost calmly, "I came to talk over the possibility of Geoffrey's — of Mr. Revian's doing a smaller copy for — for my parents. But, if he does, it will be a secret until it's finished. So — so please don't mention it to my mother."

"No, of course not," Beverley promised gravely. "What a good idea."

The other girl gave her a searching little glance, as though she might be wondering if there were a second, ironical meaning to that remark. But Beverley contrived to look guileless and friendly, and she thought she heard Sara draw a quick breath of relief.

"I must go and catch my bus now. I — I thought

I was late——" Sara glanced at her watch. "That was why I was running."

"It's all right. It doesn't go until the half-hour," Beverley assured her, with every evidence of believing her completely. "May I walk back to the bus-stop with you?" For she felt she simply could not go straight in and face Geoffrey yet, with this scene so rawly fresh in her mind.

"Why, yes — do." Sara, she saw, hardly knew whether to be relieved at the naturalness of this or distressed by the necessity of continuing to keep up appearances.

Beverley turned, and together the girls went back up the garden path.

"I missed my own bus this afternoon," Beverley said, by way of innocent conversation. "It's a maddening experience. I can imagine how anxious you were not to do the same."

"Did you? I'm so sorry. Why didn't you come back to the house? You must have been ages at the bus-stop waiting for the next bus. In fact—" Sara glanced at her companion quickly, as though any unexplained circumstance caused her alarm — "you ought to have been on the bus I took, then, surely?"

"No. I got a lift instead," Beverley explained. "I had just seen the bus drive off when a car stopped and — I was offered a lift. The driver turned out to be Mr. Lowell."

"Franklin?" Sara looked surprised and, again, vaguely alarmed. "Do you know him, then?"

"Oh, no. At least, I didn't then. I thought I recognized him from the photograph in the drawing-room which your younger sister showed me. And when I explained I had been to the Grange to arrange to do dressmaking for you all, he told me that he was engaged to you."

"Oh — I see." Sara still spoke a little hesitantly, as though she were hastily examining the circumstances and finding them fairly reassuring. "Did he drive you all the way here?"

"Yes. It was wonderful luck for me. I got home

much earlier than if I had come all round by the bus."

"I'm glad." Sara sounded genuinely so. But her tone changed again, as she said, with a not very convincingly casual air, "Where was he going, then? Surely not — here?"

"I have no idea." Beverley managed to sound cheerfully matter-of-fact. "He said something about going to Steeplemere. He stopped in Binwick only long enough to drop me at my house."

"I see." said Sara again. And this time there was no mistaking the relief in her voice.

They had reached the bus-stop by now, and Beverley stood there for a few minutes longer, in friendly conversation. Then the bus came up, and the girls said a pleasant goodbye to each other. Sara even smiled and waved through the window as the bus moved off. And Beverley had the impression that she was a good deal reassured, and fairly well satisfied that she had not given herself away too badly.

After all, why should she feel otherwise? She was unaware how completely Toni had set Beverley on the right track.

The question now, thought Beverley, was — what did she intend to do next? Should she assume that she had found out all it was necessary for her to know, and just go home? She could always say to her mother that there had been no answer to her knock when she had called at Geoffrey's cottage.

Or should she go and see Geoffrey, after all?

Although one part of her shrank from any interview with him, now that this unacknowledged barrier cut across their once happy relationship, a painful, restless curiosity also urged her to go. She *must* know how he looked when she told him of her unexpected connection with the Waynes. She *must* see for herself if there were anything in his manner which could possibly give a clue to his attitude towards Sara.

After all, she might think she knew about Sara's feelings. But how was she even to guess at Geoffrey's until she had seen his reactions to the mention of Sara's name?

With a curious mixture of distaste and eagerness, she retraced her steps to the cottage, and went round once more by the garden path to the studio.

When she knocked, his absorbed voice bade her, "Come in." And, suppressing a tremor of unfamiliar nervousness, she entered, trying to look exactly as she would have looked if she knew nothing at all of this new complication, and had merely come down to the studio to give him her own exciting news.

"Hello——" He glanced up from his easel, and gave her the faintly absent smile with which he often greeted her when he was busy. "I thought you might look in this evening."

"Did you?" She drew near and looked at the beautiful flower study which appeared to absorb his attention. "Isn't it getting a bit dark for working?"

"Yes. The best of the light is fading. But I'm not putting more than a touch to this." She had the odd impression that he had not been doing anything to it at all until her knock sounded. "What's the news? Any answers from the advertisement yet?"

"Yes." She forced a bright, pleased smile to her lips. "I had a very interesting reply this morning, and went for an interview this afternoon. It's all arranged. If I give satisfaction, I think I'll have a lot of nice work, for two or three months to come."

"You don't say!" He smiled at her with real interest. "All for one client?"

"Yes. At least — all for one family."

"Well, that's fine. Who are they?"

"The Waynes. Of Huntingford Grange."

She was aware that the hand which held his brush remained suspended for a second. Then he said,

"How odd! I know them quite well. I painted a portrait of the eldest girl early this year. You must have seen it. — Oh, no, it was just before you came back from London, I guess."

"Yes, it must have been." Her calmness matched his, she thought, and he could have no idea how

44

dreadfully her heart was sinking. "I heard about the portrait."

"From whom?" He gave her a quick glance, and she saw that his attractive dark eyes — which she had always thought before were so open and candid — were slightly narrowed.

"Oddly enough, from her fiancé, Franklin Lowell. He gave me a lift back home in his car, and he mentioned your work."

"Did he?" said Geoffrey flatly.

"Yes. And he told me that it was he who bought that first picture of yours, Geoffrey. The — the portrait of me in the blue and white frock."

"Yes. That's right." He sounded depressingly without interest in that.

"You never told me."

"No? I don't know that there was any reason why I should. He was only a name. And not a name that I specially wanted to talk about."

"Why not? Don't you like him?"

"No," said Geoffrey without elaboration.

She must have looked rather grave — possibly even a little disapproving — for after a moment he said with a smile, "Why? Should I?"

"N-no. There's no reason why you should, of course. Except that he appreciates your work. And — I thought he was quite a nice fellow myself."

The moment she had used the words she realized they in no way described Franklin Lowell. He was not "quite" or "rather" anything. There was nothing qualified or moderate about him. She supposed one would always either like him very much or dislike him intensely.

Geoffrey seemed disinclined to continue the subject of Franklin Lowell. And after a short pause she said,

"I met all three of the Wayne girls. I thought them charming."

"Yes? Sara is the only one I know really well." He said that with amazing coolness. "Although I have met all the family at various times."

"She's — lovely, isn't she?"

"Yes. She was fun to paint."

Perhaps if she had not had the key to the situation Beverley might not have guessed, even then, that he was dissembling. But, knowing what she did, she was keenly aware that he was being *too* casual — *too* objective about Sara Wayne. And suddenly it became unbearable to her that Geoffrey and she should be telling each other less than the truth.

There had always been — or so she had supposed — the happiest, most open relationship between them. That there should now be reservations — even a degree of deception — was so dreadful that she felt the tears come into her eyes, and she turned away and pretended to be examining some other picture on the other side of the studio.

She had no wish to prolong this scene. Indeed, she almost had the impulse to rush from the place. And, as soon as she had recovered herself sufficiently to trust her voice, she said,

"I mustn't stay, Geoffrey. I have to make quite an early start in the morning. But I just wanted to come down and tell you my news."

"I'm glad you did." He did not try to detain her, she noticed. "You should be quite happy working at the Grange. And——" he paused, and she thought the faintest note of bitterness crept into his voice — "with a wedding in the offing, you'll have plenty of work."

"That's what I thought," Beverley said. Then she bade him a hasty goodnight and fled.

All the way up the village street she had difficulty in restraining her tears. But she resolutely kept a cheerful, normal appearance. For there was no saying whom she might meet, or who might be gazing abstractedly from their front windows, to see how the world was faring.

She got past with no need for more than a couple of goodnights, called out to neighbours on the other side of the road, and by the time she reached home she was in full control of herself once more.

During the rest of the evening she contrived to be

her usual good-humoured self to her mother and her aunt, and it surprised neither of them that she chose to go to bed rather early.

"You want to be nice and fresh for your first day tomorrow, dear," her mother said. While Aunt Ellen remarked what a dreadful thing it would be if she missed her bus and was late the very first morning.

Alone in her own room at last, Beverley faced the future, in its new and disquieting terms. And, although the impulse to shed tears had now passed, she felt dreadfully unhappy.

It was useless to tell herself that, in practical fact, Sara Wayne was engaged to someone other than Geoffrey — indeed, to someone who would not be at all the kind to have any nonsense from a vacillating fiancée. The one inescapable conclusion which had come to her out of the muddled impressions of the day was that she herself was no longer *the* girl in Geoffrey's life.

The next morning, in spite of Aunt Ellen's anxious expectations to the contrary, Beverley caught her bus in good time, and was walking up the lane to Huntingford Grange, in the bright June sunshine, soon after half-past nine.

It was impossible not to feel cheered and even elated by the beauty of the morning. And, after being kindly received and comfortably installed in her workroom, Beverley felt bound to admit to herself that the world still had some bright spots in it. She even dared to hope that, in some as yet unexplained way, everything would somehow turn out as she wished it would.

She had been ready to start immediately on a couple of informal day dresses for Sara. But it appeared that the morning's post had brought an invitation which called for some rearrangement of work.

"Old Lady Welman is organizing a charity dance for All Saints Hospital," Mrs. Wayne explained. "I think, myself, that she has left herself *much* too little time," she added, consulting the letter in her hand, "but that's up to her. It is on the last day of the month, and she wants both the older girls to go, of course. Do you think we can manage dresses for both of them in the time?"

"Oh, yes, certainly." Beverley was confident of that. "Unless they want something extremely elaborate."

"No. Just something elegant and summery and suitable to a fairly big country-house dance. I don't think either of them has anything left over from the winter dance season which would quite fill the bill."

Sara and Madeleine came in just then and joined the discussion. And this time, Beverley noticed, Sara showed a good deal more interest in what she was to wear. In fact, she was quite firm about her choice of material, among the wealth that was available. And Beverley had to agree that nothing could have been more becoming than the exquisitely flower-patterned chiffon which she chose.

"There must be a dozen yards of it or more—" she tossed the lovely, feather-light silk upon the big table — "and I want it with a very simply draped bodice and an enormous skirt — and taffeta underneath, of course, to give it body."

Beverley promised that it should be exactly as Sara wanted it, and then she turned to Madeleine. The younger girl had more sophisticated taste, but she knew exactly what suited her, and Beverley saw that she was going to be exceptionally easy to work for.

During the afternoon Toni came up to talk and enquire. She mourned once more about having nothing to wear at Wendy Tulley's birthday party. But when she learned that Beverley would probably be able to manage something for her, as well as for the older girls, she became extremely cheerful.

Indeed, so different was she from the worried little girl who had confided her cares to Beverley the previous day that Beverley once more found her spirits swinging to the other extreme, and her hopes rising to a point from which it seemed quite credible that Toni's confidences of the day before might, after all, be largely romancing. And, that being so, was it not possible that she herself had exaggerated and misinterpreted her impressions of Sara and Geoffrey the previous evening?

She could not entirely reassure herself upon this latter point. But she did feel considerably less depressed on the general subject of Geoffrey and her connection with him.

From time to time, one or other of the Waynes would come in — either to see how she was getting on or, Beverley was rather touched to realize, merely to see that she was not lonely.

"I suppose you really like your work very much," Madeleine said to her. "You wouldn't have chosen to do anything so individual otherwise."

"I love it," Beverley replied frankly. "I wouldn't do anything else for the world."

"No?" Madeleine laughed, a half-amused, half-discontented laugh. "It must be fun to have a job — and be independent of everyone."

"Well — yes." Beverley was astonished at what seemed to her a singularly naïve and early-Victorian remark. For surely *anyone* who wanted to have a job could do so nowadays. And, after a moment, she added diffidently, "Do you mean that you would like to do the same?"

"Not dressmaking. I wouldn't be any good at that."

"No — I didn't mean dressmaking particularly. I meant — anything. Whatever you feel you have a talent for."

"I have only one talent," Madeleine said. "I'd like to go on the stage."

"Oh——" Beverley looked doubtful. She thought this too a naïve remark, because usually one passed through the phase of being stage-struck at a much earlier age. "It's a pretty hard life, even if you are talented, you know," she said diplomatically at last.

"Yes, of course. But I don't think a hard life matters if you're doing the one thing you want, do you?"

"In general — no," Beverley admitted. "But, if you feel so strongly about it, why don't you get your parents to let you have an experimental year at a drama school? That at least would show if you had enough talent to go on, or if you must resign yourself to being no more than a clever amateur."

Madeleine looked at her and laughed with real amusement.

"It sounds so simple, put that way," she said, quite good-humouredly, but this time she sounded as though *she* thought *Beverley* naïve. "My father simply wouldn't hear of it."

By now, Beverley was finding the Waynes so much like people in a book that she would not have been surprised to hear that Mr. Wayne considered the theatre a sink of iniquity and that any daughter of his who went on the stage would be told not to darken his doorstep again.

However, the truth turned out to be a little less dramatic than that.

"I suppose if we lived in London there wouldn't have been any marked opposition to our following out any experiment of the sort," Madeleine said. "But, as it is, if any of us left home, we should have to be maintained rather expensively wherever we chose to study. And, frankly—" she shrugged and laughed — "this isn't a family with very much money."

"I — see." Beverley felt faintly embarrassed, and hoped she had not sounded as though she were inviting confidences about the family's situation.

However, Madeleine went on, quite candidly.

"In addition, Father is the kind to think that pretty girls — in fact, any sort of girls — should want nothing more than to marry what he would regard as the right sort of man."

"It's quite an agreeable fate," Beverley said soberly.

"Oh, yes — I daresay." Again Madeleine shrugged. "But — there are so many other things in the world, aren't there?" And she stretched her arms above her head, as though she were literally reaching for some delectable fate just out of her range.

"I don't know. — Yes, of course, I suppose there are," Beverley agreed. "It's difficult to discuss things from two such different points of view. I belong to people who always had to accept the fact that everyone started to earn a living as soon as it was practically possible."

"My dear—" Madeleine laughed again with the utmost good-humour — "I come from people who *ought* to have realized that fact. You haven't met my father yet, have you?"

Beverley said she had not.

"He's a darling, of course," Madeleine said unexpectedly, "but the most unpractical creature on God's earth. You mustn't think I'm criticizing him. Only there are certain disadvantages to having a charming parent who belongs, in all essentials, to a past age."

Beverley said tactfully that she supposed there must be.

"Still—" Madeleine was essentially cheerful and hopeful evidently — "things have a way of working out all right in the end, haven't they? Once Sara is married to Franklin, and Andrew has found himself a niche in my uncle's firm, I daresay the parents will feel a bit more relaxed about Toni and me. I'm not saying much until my time comes. I don't know really," she added with some surprise, "why I've said so much to you."

"Probably because I am outside the family circle," Beverley told her, "and look reasonably discreet."

"*Are* you discreet?" enquired Madeleine curiously.

"As the grave," said Beverley solemnly. "Though you were not to know that." And both girls laughed and exchanged a glance of instinctive and mutual liking.

In the ensuing week, Beverley found that this first day at Huntingford Grange was a fairly good sample of those which were to follow. Mrs. Wayne was courteous and considerate, without being intimate. But the three girls — particularly Madeleine and Toni — were inclined to regard her very much as one of themselves, and to consider her an acquisition to the household.

Toni went to school — with a marked lack of enthusiasm — each day in Castleton. She had been enjoying a long half-term week-end when Beverley first met her, but now reverted to what she considered to be a brutal and exacting imposition on her free time. However, she usually returned in time to have a talk with Beverley in the late afternoon.

She never again mentioned her sister's engagement, and on the one occasion that Beverley saw Franklin Lowell at the Grange, he seemed on very good terms with everyone. Indeed, the rôle of rich but unwanted suitor appeared anything but appropriate. Except that Beverley could not detect any signs of loving, uninhibited familiarity in Sara's manner to him. But then — perhaps that was not her way.

She seemed genuinely interested when her fiancé claimed acquaintance with Beverley — who had been passing through the hall just as he came in — and said,

"Did you know that Miss Farman was the model for that painting I have of the little girl in the blue and white dress?"

"Why — no." Sara turned wide, interested eyes on Beverley. "The early Geoffrey Revian, you mean?"

"Yes."

"Then you must have known Geoffrey a long time," was what she said to Beverley.

"Since I was about twelve." Beverley contrived to make that sound casual and natural. "We've lived in the same village for years, you know."

"Oh, yes. Of course." Sara smiled sweetly, but a little vaguely. And Beverley found herself wondering what was really going on in her mind and heart, behind that cool and slightly enigmatic exterior.

"I have promised to take Miss Farman over to see the picture again, one of these days," Franklin Lowell remarked. "You will have to come too, Sara, and do the honours of the place."

Sara again smiled and said, "Yes — of course." And then Beverley had to hurry to catch her bus, and the chance encounter was over.

But seeing the two together inevitably set her wondering once more what the real situation was.

And partly because this made her restless and un-happy — and partly because it was her usual habit to go in and see him fairly often — she decided to look in and have a talk with Geoffrey again that evening.

It had been a warm day, but as she walked down the street to his cottage, a fresh evening breeze had sprung up, which seemed to lighten the slight depression which had settled on her since she had seen Sara and Franklin Lowell together.

Geoffrey was in the garden when she arrived there, lounging comfortably in a deck-chair. And although he had a sketching block on his knee and a pencil in his hand, it was obvious that he was amusing himself, rather than engaging in any serious or concentrated work.

"Hello, there." He gave her his quick, friendly smile, which always seemed to her to give such warmth to his dark eyes, and to make one feel that there was no one else in the world he would rather see. "Come and sit down and tell me your news. Will you have a drink?"

"Only if it's lemonade or something cooling." Beverley subsided into the other deck-chair and relaxed happily.

"I'll get you some lemonade." He got up.

"Oh, don't bother——" But he had already started towards the cottage, and, looking after the tall, well set-up figure in grey slacks and a blue shirt, she thought how pleasant it was to have Geoffrey perform even this small service for her.

He returned almost immediately with her drink, and stood smiling down at her while she sipped it.

"Have you been taking time off to make a new dress for yourself?" he asked. "That green is extra-ordinarily becoming."

"Is it?" She smiled and flushed. Though at one time she would have taken Geoffrey's careless compliments in her stride. "No, it's not new. I had it last year. But it's the first time I've worn it here."

"It's nice." He gave it his emphatic approval. "Like its wearer." And he ruffled her fair hair.

It was a gesture he had used sometimes when she was much younger. But certainly since she had come back from London he had not treated her with such easy-going, affectionate approval, and suddenly Beverley felt her heart begin to beat heavily.

She looked quite calm, however, as she smiled and said,

"Thank you, kind sir. Don't you want to hear about my first days at Huntingford Grange?"

"Yes, of course. They aren't working you too hard, I hope."

"Oh, no. Though we started with a bit of a rush, because both the older girls — Madeleine and — Sara—" she got the name out with a hardly perceptible pause — "are going to a big charity dance at the end of the month, and they want new dresses."

"Lady Welman's affair, I suppose?"

"Why, yes." She looked surprised. "How did you know?"

"I do hear of some of the social highlights of the local season," he assured her, with a grin. "Besides — I rather thought of going."

"Of — going, Geoffrey?" She was astounded, for she had never known him bother about any such thing.

"Yes. And of taking you too," he added.

"Of taking — *me?* Are you crazy, Geoffrey? What's come over you?"

"Nothing. What's crazy about wanting to go to a dance and take one's nicest girl friend with one?"

She was dumb for a moment. Partly at this description of her, partly with astonishment at this sudden and totally unexpected interest in social affairs.

"Wouldn't you like to come?" he pressed her.

"In a way — yes. Immensely! But—" she bit her lip doubtfully — "it's a little awkward, with the Wayne girls going."

"Why should it be? Anyone who likes to buy a ticket in aid of All Saints can go."

"Yes, of course. But — though they are terribly friendly and nice to me while I'm there — I'm really just the girl who makes their dresses," Beverley said a little anxiously.

"Don't be an inverted snob," Geoffrey retorted. "I'm just the chap that painted Sara Wayne's portrait, come to that."

Beverley laughed.

"That's quite different," she said. "I wouldn't like them to think that I was trying to — to worm my way into the same social life as they have, just because I've come to know them as clients."

"They wouldn't be so stupid as to think anything of the sort. You will be there as my partner."

"But they might think — at least, Mrs. Wayne might think — that I had persuaded you to take me, so that I could push my way into what is much more their circle than mine."

"Don't you believe it!" Geoffrey laughed, and suddenly he put out his hand and drew her to her feet, so that she was close against him for a moment. "They will understand exactly why you are there with me, my dear little goose. Because you are going to get engaged to me beforehand, and go with me as my fiancée," he told her.

CHAPTER FOUR

FOR A wild, improbable moment, it seemed to Beverley that the setting sun rushed up the sky again and shone in fullest glory.

She could not — she *could* not, she thought — have heard Geoffrey aright. And yet how could she have mistaken such wonderful, pregnant words? He had smiled as he said them, it was true, and he was looking teasing and indulgent now. But then that was often Geoffrey's way. To say something of importance, with an air of amused casualness which gave it a delicious novelty.

"Well—" he touched her cheek with gentle fingers — "no comment?"

"I—" she turned and hugged him suddenly — "Geoffrey, did I really hear what I thought I heard?"

"If you heard me say we are engaged — then it's all right," he told her with a grin.

"But — without the slightest warning — without any preparation — how *could* you? How do you expect me to be anything but stunned?"

He laughed.

"Haven't you noticed in the last ten years, that I'm extremely fond of you?" he enquired.

"Of course. But——" She was silent suddenly. For — she could not have said why — she was strangely and disagreeably struck by his exact choice of phrase.

"Extremely fond of her" might most properly describe the various degrees of affection he had felt for her from the time she was a child until he asked her to marry him, of course. But why could he not have said that he loved her? *That* was what she wanted to hear.

Extremely fond! An expression one used to other people, besides the one girl of one's heart. Why, it was the expression one might use to someone who was — second best.

"Geoffrey—" she put her hands flat against him,

56

almost as though she would have pushed him away — "why did you say just that?"

"Just what, darling?"

"That you were extremely fond of me."

"Because I am." He looked amused and puzzled.

"But — I'd rather you said that you — that you love me. It — means more."

"Then I love you, my dearest child. Do you need to be reassured of the fact?"

She did. That was exactly the case, of course. And yet she felt almost ungenerous as the idea came to her. This was the moment of her life. The moment she had hoped for during more years than she could assess. Was she to spoil it now because of some melodramatic misunderstanding implanted in her mind by an over-talkative child?

"Oh, Geoffrey—" she pressed her fair head against his shoulder in an access of affection — "it's so wonderful that I can't take it in yet. How could you lead up to it so casually, just by way of Lady Welman's silly dance?"

"It isn't a silly dance. It's rather a swell affair," he told her, as he dropped a kiss on the top of her head. "And you mustn't disparage it, if we're going to appear there for the first time in public together as an engaged couple. I take it you *are* coming with me now?"

"Why — of course. *Everything* is all right now!"

Even as she said that, she wondered if it were quite true. But what could be wrong, if Geoffrey had asked her to marry him?

"When did you first think of — of doing this?" she asked, half-diffidently.

"Of going to the dance?" he asked teasingly.

"No. Of marrying me."

"About eight years ago. When I first did that portrait of you in the blue and white dress."

"Oh, Geoffrey!" She was enchanted, and almost completely reassured.

"Then I forgot about it——"

"Oh, Geoffrey!" she said again, and this time she was not so enchanted.

"—Until quite recently. When I re-examined the idea once more—" again he gave her that teasing smile — "and found it quite a sound notion."

She laughed. She knew that she was meant to laugh, and that this was no unusual way for Geoffrey to talk. But some utterly perverse side of her kept on discovering a second, disturbing meaning in everything he said.

He had found it "a sound notion" to propose marriage to her. Why?

"Are you really so surprised that I want you to marry me?" he asked her at that moment. "You reacted as though nothing were further from your thoughts. Did you never think, in all the years we have known each other, that it was the logical — almost the inevitable — conclusion?"

"Yes," she said quietly and frankly, "I did think so sometimes. I — it doesn't matter my saying so now — I hoped so. But you told me once, years ago, that you couldn't ever afford to marry."

"Well, I suppose that's still true, so far as many girls are concerned." He laughed rather shortly, she thought. "Maybe some people would say I oughtn't to ask you now, Beverley. I haven't a great deal to offer you, in the worldly sense."

"It doesn't matter," she said quickly. "You'll be a success one day, I *know*. And, even if you're not, I still don't mind."

"You're a darling." He held her close and kissed her, with an odd touch of something like remorse. Perhaps because he felt that for her sake he should abandon his artistic struggles and accept the humdrum prosperity which his father still offered. "I'm not really half good enough for you, you know," he exclaimed.

"That's for me to say, isn't it?" She smiled up at him.

"I don't know. Perhaps I'm being a selfish hound

in asking you." And for a moment he looked sombre, and somehow a good deal older than his age.

"No, you're not. You are making me very happy," Beverley told him. "And no man can do more for a girl than that."

He laughed at that and kissed her again.

"Then we're engaged?" he said.

"Yes — we're engaged," she repeated slowly. "I couldn't — have imagined — such a thing, when I came down here this evening."

"Shall I walk back with you and tell your mother now?" he asked. "Or would you like to wait to tell people until you have your ring?"

"I don't specially want to wait. I — I don't even mind if I don't have a ring. Or only a very modest one," she said earnestly. For it seemed to her that the provision of an expensive ring might present a problem for Geoffrey, whom she still regarded as a struggling artist.

However, he was emphatic about the necessity of a ring.

"Of course you will have one! Either you can have one of your own choice, or else you can have the very beautiful ring which my grandmother left me, among her other possessions. It would need resetting, I daresay. But it has a very fine diamond in it, and a couple of sapphires, if I remember rightly."

Beverley said that she would love to have his grandmother's ring. And indeed it seemed to her that, in owning a family ring, she would feel a sense of permanence and continuity in her link with Geoffrey which was just what her heart craved.

"Then come on indoors now, and I'll show it to you," he said. And arm-in-arm they went into the house.

The ring, which he produced from a concealed drawer in his writing-desk, proved to be beautiful and obviously of value. The setting, however, was rather heavy and old-fashioned, and Geoffrey immediately began to make a sketch of how he thought it should be reset.

She hung over, watching him, so close that her hair brushed against his cheek. And once he turned his head and kissed her.

"There — how do you like that?" He held out the sketch for her approval.

"It's wonderful. It makes it more *my* ring."

"Then I'll take it into Castleton tomorrow," Geoffrey said. "And I'll insist that they have it ready at any rate in time for you to wear it at the dance."

Her eyes sparkled.

"Shall we — keep the news of our engagement to ourselves until then?" she suggested. For suddenly she felt nervous at the thought of having to mention her news perhaps at Huntingford Grange on the morrow.

"If you like. Except that I think we should tell your mother."

"Oh, of course!" Beverley agreed.

And so presently they strolled back to Beverley's home together, to break the happy news to her mother and her aunt.

Mrs. Farman had, of course, known Geoffrey well for years. And, looking at her daughter's flushed and happy face, she expressed the utmost pleasure over the engagement. And even Aunt Ellen — though she looked unsuitably glum — produced some delicious home-made wine, in which to drink a toast to the occasion.

For half an hour Geoffrey stayed, while they talked happy generalities. Then he said goodnight and went away, leaving Beverley to the more particular questions and comments of her mother and her aunt.

"I suppose," Mrs. Farman said pensively, "that I ought to have asked him if he could provide properly for you, and so on. Since your father is no longer here, maybe that was my business. But — it seems out of date, somehow, to ask these things nowadays, when young people make up their minds first — very properly — and tell their parents afterwards."

"Oh, it's very out of date," Beverley assured her hastily.

"It is, however, very practical and to the point," said Aunt Ellen. "*Can* he provide properly for you?"

"I suppose it depends what you mean by providing for someone," Beverley replied dryly.

"I mean what the expression has always meant," Aunt Ellen stated obstinately. "Can he assure you a home and an income on which you can both live in reasonable comfort, according to what you've been used to?"

"He has a home — as you know," Beverley said rather coldly.

"That tumbledown cottage?" Aunt Ellen sniffed eloquently. "*I* wouldn't want to live there."

Beverley was sorely tempted to observe that no one had invited her to do so. But she bit her lip, in order to keep silent, and her mother said pacifically,

"It will be wonderful to have you so near, darling. Have you made any plans yet about — about *when* you intend to marry?"

"Oh, no!" To Beverley the idea of being engaged to Geoffrey was, in itself, so difficult to believe that she could not yet go on confidently to contemplate the particular circumstances of married life with him.

"Will you go on working?" enquired Aunt Ellen, who had a great talent for asking the things that were better left unasked.

"I suppose so. In fact — yes, of course I shall. Why not?"

Aunt Ellen did not answer that in words, but she shook her head and sighed, which Beverley found so exasperating that, if she had not caught her mother's amused and sympathetic glance, she would probably have been really rude to her aunt at that moment.

However, nothing could cloud her spirits for long. Not even the faint undefined sensation of worry which lingered still in the background of her mind because of what Toni Wayne had said.

With all her common sense and determination she suppressed that occasional quiver of anxiety. For in what way could the melodramatic confidences of an imaginative little girl count against the solid, wonderful fact that Geoffrey had asked her to marry him?

She slept dreamlessly that night, and woke to a glorious morning which seemed a fitting accompaniment to the radiant discovery which broke afresh upon her as she rose to consciousness.

"I'm engaged to Geoffrey!" she thought, as she opened her eyes to the sunlight which was pouring in through the bedroom window. "He asked me to marry him. There is nothing to worry about any more. I'm engaged — to Geoffrey."

Oddly enough, she had no special urge to share this wonderful fact with anyone — no special temptation to tell anyone she knew who was with her on the bus that morning. It was enough that she knew about it herself, and could hug to her the heavenly knowledge that, even that very day, Geoffrey would go into Castleton to have his grandmother's ring reset as her own engagement ring.

As she walked up the lane to Huntingford Grange, her new inner happiness tended to be slightly overcast by the strong impressions which she associated with the Grange. Somehow, it was not so easy in this setting to be *sure* that Toni had been wrong in her conjectures or to *know* that Geoffrey loved her, and had loved her for years.

On the contrary, she thought — with disquieting clarity — of how Sara had run from Geoffrey's studio, flushed and agitated, and with every air of having passed through some emotional scene. And she asked herself how she was to reconcile this with the coolness of Geoffrey's own references to Sara, and the fact that she herself was the girl he had asked to marry him.

Fortunately a very busy day lay ahead of Beverley. And not only was there no question of her talking to anyone about her own affairs — even had she wished to do so, which she did not — but, in addition, she even had very little time to think about them herself.

Towards the end of the afternoon, however, the

dance dresses for Sara and Madeleine had progressed as far as a final fitting. And the unfeigned delight of the two girls with her work certainly warmed Beverley's heart.

"You clever, clever girl!" cried Madeleine, with generous enthusiasm. "I simply adore this uncluttered line. I don't know when I've looked so good in anything."

"You're much too beautiful ever to look less than good," Beverley assured her frankly. "But I do agree that this particular style brings out all your best points."

"Isn't it wonderful, Mother?" Madeleine turned eagerly to her mother, who had come in to watch and to appraise while the last fitting was made.

"Very beautiful," Mrs. Wayne agreed, in an extremely satisfied tone. "You couldn't have done better, Miss Farman. And, Sara dear, you were quite right to have that chiffon. Franklin will love you in all that floral femininity."

"I hope he will love me in anything," retorted Sara, but a trifle carelessly. "I'm delighted with it, though, Miss Farman. You have even a touch of genius, I think."

It was impossible not to be delighted with all these compliments. And Beverley felt so happy and so well disposed towards them all that she almost became expansive enough, on her side, to tell them her own good news.

But some lingering doubt of the way they might receive this held her back. And so she just smiled, and coloured slightly and becomingly, and said she was very glad indeed that they were all so pleased.

"I think Toni's party dress is going to be lovely too," she added, as that young woman came bounding in, just returned from school. And, at Toni's urgent and rather maddeningly reiterated requests, this dress also was tried on and pronounced ideal.

"You *are* clever, Miss Farman. I think you ought to have a specially nice tea, as a reward," declared Toni. And although they all laughed a good deal at this point of view, Beverley had the conviction that there would be no querying of her "high prices," when her bill came in.

Perhaps Toni was not the only one who felt vaguely that some special acknowledgement of the first success would not be out of place. At any rate, just as Beverley was thinking of packing away her work for the day, Sara came upstairs again and put her head round the door.

"Miss Farman, are you in any special hurry to get home? Because Franklin — Mr. Lowell — has just come, to drive me over to his place to see about some alterations which the builders have been doing. And he suggests that you might like to take the opportunity of coming to see your portrait."

"Why — how kind of you!"

Beverley was a good deal touched by the friendliness of the gesture, and the fact that Sara, as well as Franklin Lowell, seemed to think it was perfectly natural to change a casual suggestion into a definite invitation.

"I'd love to come," Beverley admitted. "I'll be ready in five minutes."

"All right. Come down when you're ready. You'll find us in the little drawing-room," Sara told her.

She went away again, and Beverley hurried with her clearing-up operations. The invitation was very welcome, in more ways than one. Quite apart from the fact that it would really be delightfully interesting to see Geoffrey's picture of her once more, she thought suddenly that the chance of seeing Sara and Franklin Lowell together in their future home might do more for her than anything else to set her mind finally at rest about Toni's confidences.

She might, once and for all, see that Sara's apparent indifference was no more than a reserved manner. And she might conceivably find, in the contemplation of the two of them together, something entirely reassuring to set against that disagreeable recollection of Sara outside Geoffrey's studio.

When she came downstairs, she found not only

Franklin Lowell and all the members of the Wayne family whom she already knew, but also, for the first time, Mr. Wayne.

He had, she had gathered, been away on some vague business trip abroad during her first week or so at Huntingford Grange. But now that she saw him, she remembered immediately what his second daughter had said about his being a darling but quite unpractical. And she thought that, whatever his trip abroad had included, good, hard, practical business affairs had not been to the fore.

He was an exceptionally handsome man — it was obvious where the Wayne girls got their looks — and he had a genial, charming, all-embracing manner which was in curious contrast to his wife's cool reserve. On being introduced to Beverley, he welcomed her more as a friend of the family than a casual employee, and she very much doubted if he had even noticed the few words of explanation with which Mrs. Wayne had amplified the introduction.

All he appeared to have caught was the fact that she came from Binwick, and he immediately launched into an eloquent appreciation of the beauties and the historical significance of Binwick, delivered in a rich and flexible voice to which one could only listen with admiration and pleasure.

His manner was rather that of a slightly old-fashioned but highly gifted actor-manager, and Beverley could not help thinking that if Madeleine had any grounds for visualizing herself succeeding in a stage career, she must have inherited these from her father.

He seemed to be on unexpectedly good terms with his future son-in-law. And, if Franklin Lowell listened to the dissertation on Binwick with obvious amusement, it was a sort of indulgent amusement. At the end, he got to his feet, stretched himself lazily, so that Beverley could not help noticing how tall and strangely graceful he was, and said,

"Well, shall we go now?"

In contrast to Mr. Wayne's rolling periods, there

was something almost comic about the curt economy of that.

But Sara, it seemed, was quite ready to go. She said goodbye to her mother and went out to the car with Franklin — Beverley following a tactful step or two behind.

Just as they had seated themselves, however, Sara remembered that she had forgotten something she wanted to take over to Franklin's housekeeper.

"I won't be a minute," she promised. "Wait for me." And, jumping out of the car, she ran into the house once more.

It was very pleasant, sitting out there in the late afternoon sunshine, the windows of the car open to the breeze which almost always blew round the small plateau on which Huntingford Grange was built. And leaning back in her seat, Beverley relaxed with a slight, contented sigh.

Franklin Lowell turned round in the driving-seat and smiled at her.

"Settling down all right here?" he enquired good-humouredly.

"Oh, yes, indeed! Everyone is very kind to me. And they are a delightful — an interesting family to work for."

"Yes, they're interesting, all right. Is that the first time you've met Mr. Wayne?"

Beverley said it was.

"Amazing fellow." Franklin Lowell grinned reminiscently. "Now my old man wouldn't have managed to say as much as that about the place where he was born and bred. And I don't expect Mr. Wayne has passed through Binwick more than a dozen times in the car. You would think he'd left half his heart there."

Beverley laughed.

"He has a wonderful speaking voice," she said sincerely.

"Yes. I suppose he's what you mean by a spellbinder," her companion agreed, but without rancour.

"They all have a touch of it. I think that's why they fascinate me as a family."

"Do they fascinate you?" Beverley was interested, and a little amused to hear him admit to that. "I mean — I understand that your fiancée fascinates you, naturally. But — as a family?"

"Yes. The whole lot of them. Even Toni. There is nothing the least bit standardized about them, in an increasingly standardized world. Sometimes I don't think I understand any of them. Not even Sara. Perhaps least of all Sara," he added, half to himself.

But before Beverley could ask him what he meant by that — if, indeed, she could have done so in any case — Sara herself came out of the house again and rejoined them.

"I'm sorry. I hope I didn't keep you too long."

"It's all right." Franklin smiled at her, with an air of affectionate indulgence which Beverley found charming.

They drove off then. And, sitting there in the back seat of the car, Beverley unobtrusively watched the other two, as they chatted to each other in front. Once or twice Sara turned round and included Beverley in the conversation. But mostly she and Franklin appeared to be talking about the structural alterations they were going to see.

In a sense they were on good terms, Beverley supposed. That was to say they seemed to agree quite pleasantly about what should still be done, and several times he turned to flash that singularly attractive smile at Sara. And yet — all that Beverley could say to herself was that *she* would have felt and behaved quite differently if she had been driving out with Geoffrey to inspect their future home.

But this, she reminded herself, could be quite easily explained by the difference in temperament between her and Sara Wayne. Why *should* Sara be eager and expansive and excited, if that were not her disposition?

The drive took less than twenty minutes and brought them to Elthorpe Hall, which had, Beverley remembered, been inhabited during most of her growing-up years by an elderly recluse who had died about five years previously.

"Why, I didn't realize you lived here!" she said to Franklin Lowell. "It was empty for several years, wasn't it?"

"Yes. I bought it about a year ago. And now Sara and I are gradually having it changed to suit our future plans."

"Then my portrait — I mean the picture of me — hasn't been hanging here long?"

"Oh, no. I had it in my flat in London."

"In your flat?"

"Yes. Why·not?" He glanced round, rather amused, she realized.

"Oh, I — don't know," Beverley said. But what she was really thinking was that there was something extraordinarily intimate about living with a portrait in a flat. Even a big flat. And even if the portrait were of a little girl.

In a big country house one might not notice it for days on end. It might even become part of the general surroundings. But in a flat, somehow, it was like a day-to-day personal contact. She thought she saw now why he had spoken of her picture as "my little girl in the blue and white frock" in that half-amused, half-fanciful way. And the reflection curiously touched her.

When they came into the big panelled entrance hall of the house, the very correct and elderly housekeeper came out to greet them, and almost immediately Sara excused herself and went off with her.

"Show Miss Farman her picture," she said to Franklin over her shoulder. "I shan't be long."

And so, rather to Beverley's pleasure, she and Franklin Lowell went off together to look at her picture.

It was hanging, in an excellent light, in a small panelled room, which had long windows opening out on to a terrace at the back of the house. There was no other picture in the room and, either because it really was very good, or because it had been very skilfully placed, it was extraordinarily effective.

"I say—" Beverley stood smilingly surveying it — "it's rather nice, isn't it?"

"It's the nicest picture I know," said Franklin Lowell.

She laughed.

"Have you told Geoffrey that?"

"No. I don't think so."

"You should do. It's an expression of opinion that any artist would like to hear passed on his work."

"I don't know that it's only the work which prompts the opinion," Franklin Lowell said. "The subject's nice too."

"Oh—" Beverley laughed again and flushed that time — "children always make effective models."

"Indeed they do not. I have seen some child studies which make me sick."

"Oh, well — haven't we all?" Beverley said feelingly. "Does Sara — does Miss Wayne like the picture?"

"Very much. I think that was why she was so eager to have Revian paint her."

"Was it?" thought Beverley. But aloud she said, "I should love to see the portrait of her, if I may."

"Yes, of course. It's in my study. Come this way."

As they crossed the hall again, Sara rejoined them and asked in such a friendly and casual way how Beverley had liked her picture that suddenly Beverley was almost sure that all her fears and imaginings were ridiculous fancy.

"I think it's enchanting. I had forgotten how well Geoffrey did it," she said. "And now I'm curious to see his portrait of you."

"Oh, yes. It's in the study." Sara came with them, to the rather austere room where it was obvious that a great deal of serious work was done.

The beautiful, curiously romantic portrait was rather out of keeping with the rest of the room. And yet its intrinsic loveliness justified its position anywhere.

"It's absolutely lovely!" Beverley exclaimed. "I

don't think even Geoffrey ever did anything better. It's exactly like you. Oh, he *is* clever!"

The others both laughed at her enthusiasm, and Sara turned once more to examine the portrait appraisingly, while Franklin said teasingly to Beverley, "You are an admirer of his, aren't you?"

"Oh, yes!" Beverley flushed again, with the intensity of her feelings. And then suddenly — she could not have said whether it was simply that she could no longer keep her news to herself, or whether it was the imperative desire to put all her doubts to the test — she looked at Sara's unconscious back and added, "As a matter of fact, I became engaged to him yesterday evening."

CHAPTER FIVE

"YOU'RE engaged?" repeated Franklin, on a note of amusement and surprise. "To Geoffrey Revian? Why, congratulations——" He held out his hand to her. "How did you keep that news to yourself until now?"

"Oh, there — there were quite a lot of other things to attend to today," she assured him, and she tried to make her voice sound naturally frank and happy. But she looked past him as she spoke, to the very still figure of Sara, who even now had not turned round.

"Did you hear that, Sara?" Franklin too looked over at his fiancée then. "Did you know about Miss Farman's engagement?"

And then, at last, Sara did turn to face them, and Beverley saw that she was very pale.

"Yes — I heard." Sara spoke in a quiet, strangely flat voice. "But I didn't know about it before. I — hope you will be very happy, Miss Farman."

"Thank you," said Beverley in a small voice, for she felt most strangely as though she had struck some unoffending person in the face.

She had not intended to hurt Sara like that. Before she spoke the fatal words, she had almost convinced herself that the other girl really had no interest in Geoffrey, after all. Now — in face of that blank look and inescapable pallor — she could no longer cherish any illusions. Whatever Geoffrey's attitude might be, there was no doubt of Sara's fondness for him.

"Aren't you well, darling?"

It was Franklin who spoke suddenly, galvanizing both girls into the realization that they must somehow disguise the immense gulf which had all at once been torn in their relationship.

"I'm all right." Sara roused herself. "I have a slight

71

headache, but it's nothing much. Don't we want to show Miss Farman the rest of the house?"

With the eager assurance that she would love to see more of Elthorpe Hall, Beverley seconded this attempt to return to normality. And, as they started on an informal tour of the house, she forced herself to make easy conversation, so as to hide the fact that Sara had become strangely silent again.

She asked Franklin all sorts of questions — how he had come to buy the place, and what other alterations he and Sara proposed to make.

"I always wanted a place of this kind," he told her candidly. "I suppose—" he grinned reflectively — "it's something in me from some farming ancestors, way back in the family. Then, when my father died, he left me a controlling interest in a variety of concerns — mostly to do with plastics. A lot of our work is done in the Tyne Valley, and it seemed the reasonable moment to combine my business interests with the pleasures of owning a country estate. Now all I need is a beautiful wife to grace the scene. Isn't that right, my sweet?" And he put his arm round Sara.

"Yes," she said. But that was all.

In other circumstances, Beverley would have been truly interested to see over Elthorpe Hall. But, as it was, she felt the strain of the present situation increasing with every room she looked at and admired.

She supposed that what she wanted more than anything else in the world was to have Sara to herself for ten minutes. And yet, even if she achieved that, what was there she could say?

In the end, the opportunity came with almost frightening suddenness and simplicity. They had all returned to the pleasant drawing-room overlooking a terraced garden where excellent coffee and sandwiches had been set out by the housekeeper. And, just as they had sat down, a servant came to say that Franklin was wanted on the telephone.

"Don't wait for me," he said. "If it's Thompson

about the new barns I may be some while." And then he went away, leaving the two girls together.

There was silence for a moment. Then Beverley, unable to sit still and exchange no more than social pleasantries, got up from her chair and walked restlessly to the window.

"May I pour you some coffee?" Sara's voice enquired politely and formally behind her.

"Yes, please — I mean — no, thank you——" Beverley turned, with sudden resolution and faced the other girl. "Never mind about the coffee for the moment." She spoke quite gently. "There's something else we must talk about."

"Are you sure?" Sara raised her beautiful eyes and looked Beverley full in the face. "Aren't some things better left unsaid?"

"Sometimes, perhaps. But not in this case." Beverley came over and sat down again, facing the other girl. "Sara——" in that moment any social distinction between them was wiped out — "I simply have to ask you something. You're in love with Geoffrey Revian yourself, aren't you?"

Even up to that very last moment, perhaps she had some wild hope that all her fears would be proved groundless. But, if so, the hope was dashed by the way Sara caught her breath at the question. There was a moment's hesitation, then she said quietly,

"Yes." Though she added almost immediately. "But it isn't any good."

"How do you mean? — it isn't any good?"

"There was never any question of our — marrying. There is no reason why you should not be engaged to him."

"But — you can't just dispose of it like that!" Beverley was aghast, both at the final confirmation of her worst fears and at Sara's over-simplification of a tragically complicated issue. "I can't possibly marry Geoffrey knowing that he — he loves someone else."

Again there was an infinitesimal pause. Then Sara spoke, with an effort, Beverley thought.

"I didn't say that he loved me. I only said I loved him."

"Oh — my dear——" Beverley put out her hand, and in that moment of compassion she felt that one was almost as much of a barrier as the other. "I'm sorry to — to make you talk of your most private feelings, but—"

"It doesn't matter. I suppose we *had* to talk of them, after what happened half an hour ago." Sara was strangely calm about it all now. "How did you — guess, by the way?"

"That you loved Geoffrey?"

"Yes."

"Oh — one or two things made me wonder—" Beverley was not going to betray Toni even now — "but only quite passingly. Then — the way you looked when I spoke of my engagement——"

"Did I give myself away *so* completely?"

"N-no. But you went white and looked — stunned."

"Do you think Franklin noticed?"

"Only enough to think you unwell. He accepted the headache excuse, I'm sure. Men are rather dense about these things," Beverley said consolingly.

"Not Franklin," replied Sara dryly, but she seemed reassured. Then she rather deliberately poured out coffee for them both and said, "Tell me about yourself and — Geoffrey."

This was not quite what Beverley had intended. She had wanted Sara to tell her about *herself* and Geoffrey. But she could not refuse to answer a request put with so little offence, even if, in a sense, she were talking to her rival.

"I've known him since I was a child — as I told you," she began hesitatingly. "I — I think I have always loved him, though not, of course, always in quite the same way, over the years. But he — he always seemed, in some way, to be — mine. I didn't often think specifically about marrying him, because I never thought of him as being in a position to marry."

"He's not, I suppose, even now," Sara remarked, with a faint smile.

"That's why I assumed there — there wouldn't be anyone else in his life." Beverley hesitated for a moment, while she reviewed the hopes and fears of the immediate past and wondered what she could venture to tell Sara. Then she saw it was impossible to enlarge on those, and she said lamely, "Then, quite unexpectedly, last night he asked me to marry him."

"Last night?" Sara spoke almost under her breath. "It was so recent? Only — last night!"

"Yes." Beverley had not meant her voice to sound forlorn, but the fearful drop from the high hopes of the previous evening to the disillusionment of the last half-hour could not be borne without a quiver in one's tone.

Perhaps that was what suddenly roused Sara to the realization that someone else's happiness was at stake.

"Listen, Beverley—" she leaned forward and put her hand on Beverley's arm — "you're not to let this interfere with your happiness — or his. As you can see, I'm going to marry someone else. I have my life mapped out in front of me. I'm sorry I hadn't the self-discipline to hide my feelings better just now — but the weakness is past. I shall marry Franklin and be a very fortunate girl in many ways, and all my family will be delighted. You will marry Geoffrey and — I beg you — forget anything that happened or was said this afternoon."

"I can't, you know," Beverley replied quite simply. "Human nature doesn't react that way."

"But what do you propose to do?" Sara opened her eyes wide.

"I don't know."

"You wouldn't be so foolish as to — to bring the subject up with Geoffrey."

"I don't know," Beverley said again. "No, I don't think so. But—" she summoned all her resolution — "Sara, there is something I simply must know, either from you or from him. You said just now that — that you loved him, but that you had made no assertion that he loved you. Did that mean—" she swallowed — "was that your way of saying that he *doesn't* love you?"

"I suppose so." Sara looked straight in front of her, rather stonily.

"But — can't you be more categorical?" cried Beverley. "Oh, I know it's awful to ask you to define his attitude, when you feel as you do. But — don't you see? — I'm tormented by the idea that he — he just decided to marry me on the rebound. I wouldn't be prepared to accept that. I'd rather——"

"Beverley—" suddenly the other girl spoke with an instinctive half-bitter sort of knowledge quite unlike her usual passionless attitude — "don't you know that things are never satisfactorily black or white in this life? I can only tell you that if Geoffrey ever loved me at all, he certainly didn't love me well enough to alter his life in the only way that would have made it possible for us to marry."

"I don't understand."

"No. How should you?" Sara passed her hand over her face, as though literally clearing away the cobwebs from her own vision. "It's not very simple to people who don't know our family well. But I'll try to explain——"

"Please do." Beverley looked at her anxiously, as though she were talking some different and not very familiar language.

"We're poor and we're ambitious, Beverley. Almost all of us — except perhaps Toni——" Sara smiled faintly. "I'm not free from the same outlook myself. I don't think I'd be prepared to be a poor man's wife, even if I were left entirely to my own choice. But whether I would or not just doesn't arise. What I do affects all the others in the family, in a lesser or greater degree. I'm almost the best asset they have—" she said it without conceit and without false modesty — "I'm the beautiful eldest daughter who always *has* to marry money——"

"But they can't——" began Beverley in horrified protest.

"Wait——" Sara held up her hand, again with that faint smile. "You mustn't think there is anything melodramatic or cruel about it. No one would actually put violent pressure on me — except emotionally speaking — if I refused to play ball. But unless I marry money, the family situation will be pretty grim. Lots of girls, I suppose, have to do the same——"

"Indeed they don't!" exclaimed Beverley, in energetic protest.

"Oh, yes, they do. Not as a clear-cut issue, perhaps. But their family needs — and, to a certain extent, their own tastes and inclinations — lead them inevitably that way. I don't mean that I would marry an odious man, just because he was rich, and no one in the family would expect me to do so——"

"I should think not, indeed!"

"But Franklin is quite a dear——" Beverley found herself hoping, passingly, that the gay, high-spirited, rather arrogant Franklin Lowell would never know that Sara spoke of him in that casual way. "He is the answer to all our prayers. I shall marry him."

"And — Geoffrey?"

"Geoffrey just wouldn't do," Sara said quietly and deliberately. "A poor, struggling artist would be nothing less than a disaster in our family."

Beverley stared at the other girl, still unable to take in completely a view of life so totally different from her own. After a moment she said slowly,

"Then you never seriously considered Geoffrey as a — a husband?" A sort of hope, undefined but real, began to stir in her heart again.

"Not as things are."

Hope died, and an acute anxiety took its place.

"You said something just now — that he wouldn't alter his life in the only way that would have made a — a marriage possible. What, exactly, did you mean by that? Did you — discuss the subject with him?"

"Oh, Beverley—" Sara shrugged, half-humourously, half-despairingly — "where is the dividing line between our hopes and our suggestions? I — let him know that I couldn't think of marrying a poor man——"

"Quite academically speaking?" interrupted Beverley sharply.

There was the faintest pause. Then Sara said, though without looking at Beverley,

"Quite academically speaking. If he wanted me enough, he must have known from that, that he would have to make things up with his father——"

"But he couldn't do that without giving up his painting!" Beverley, who had followed all the details of that struggle so sympathetically, was aghast at the idea. But Sara was less impressed.

"That was up to him," she said calmly. "He could have made a reconciliation if he wanted to. And his father is quite a wealthy man. Not so rich as Franklin, of course, but rich enough to make his only son acceptable in my family, provided they were on good terms. Geoffrey was not prepared to do that."

"Did he say as much?" Beverley asked quickly. And she almost prayed that the other girl would look her in the face when she replied, so that she would know positively and for ever if the real truth were being told.

But Sara's long lashes came down, in that faintly secretive way of hers, and her face was expressionless as she said,

"It was never discussed categorically. The facts spoke for themselves."

Beverley thought it was hopelessly, maddeningly unsatisfactory to have facts speaking for themselves. She wanted someone to say, in so many words, that, even if Geoffrey had once been very much attracted to Sara, that was over and done with, and had, in any case, never amounted to very much.

But Geoffrey was the only one who could make that categorical statement. And how could one, with any decency and dignity, ask Geoffrey?

Possibly Sara could have said more. Or possibly she chose to conceal more, both for her own self-respect and a genuine concern for Beverley's peace of mind. In any case, they seemed suddenly to have come to the end of the extraordinary flood of candour which had broken loose over them, and now they sat silently facing each other over the coffee and sandwiches.

So they were sitting when Franklin came back again, with apologies for having left them so long.

If he detected any strain in their manner, he concealed the fact admirably and, with a tremendous effort, Beverley once more contrived to take a reasonable part in the conventional conversation which filled the gap until it was time to go.

At this point Sara pleaded that her headache had become worse, and asked if Beverley would mind their dropping her first at Huntingford Grange before making the journey to Binwick.

"No, of course not." Beverley tried to look completely convinced of the genuineness of this excuse, while Franklin Lowell, in the manner of most thoroughly healthy people faced by even a minor indisposition in someone else, looked rather nonplussed.

"It's nothing, really," Sara explained almost impatiently. "I'll be all right in the morning."

And so they drove back to Huntingford Grange, where Sara bade them both a very brief goodnight and left them.

"You had better come and sit in front now," Franklin suggested to Beverley, when Sara had disappeared into the house. "It's more companionable that way."

So Beverley changed her seat. And presently when the somewhat sobering effect of Sara's pale presence had passed, her companion began to ask her in a friendly way about her own affairs — when she and Geoffrey hoped to get married and what their future plans might be.

Somehow, it was much easier explaining the position to Franklin Lowell than to Aunt Ellen, and

Beverley found herself telling him quite frankly that they had not been able to get very far yet with the practical arrangements.

"Just made the one big discovery that you were born for each other, and left it at that?" he suggested.

"More or less." She tried not to think of what Sara and she had discussed that evening. "Though, of course," she went on, with a slight effort, "we have known each other for so long that it couldn't really have come as a complete surprise to us — both."

"But it was a surprise to you?" He was, she realized, quick to sense shades of meaning in a doubtful tone.

"In the end — yes." And then, in a sort of burst of confidence she said, "Sometimes one hopes for a long time, without really daring to expect anything to happen. And then — suddenly — it happens."

"And that was the way with you?" He smiled, not unkindly. "So that now all the anxiety and doubts are over, eh?"

She didn't answer. Because, when the situation was put into words like that, she was overwhelmed by the thought of the anxiety and doubts which still remained.

Apparently he was good at interpreting silences too, for he gave her that shrewd, oddly friendly glance and said,

"Not quite over, I see. What's the trouble?"

"There — there isn't any," she declared quickly, startled that he could read her so easily.

He did not press the point, and she could have left the matter there. But something — perhaps it was the unspeakable urge to be reassured by someone, anyone — goaded her into further, inexplicable confidences.

"I don't know why I'm telling you — but, for a while, I — I thought he was keen on someone else."

"Well, it seems you were wrong," he pointed out philosophically.

"I — don't know."

He glanced at her again. Then he said in a deliberately matter-of-fact sort of voice,

"Lots of men have a preliminary flutter with someone else before they settle down with the one girl who matters."

"I know. I suppose it's — silly to worry."

"Very," he assured her, but again not unkindly. "Concentrate on what is coming, my dear, not on what is past. Are you going to settle in Binwick?"

"Oh, yes!" She explained briefly about her mother. "And I shall go on working too. We shan't be too well off," she admitted, with a candour which seemed to amuse him.

"No? And yet—" he frowned consideringly — "Revian ought to make money, you know. He's got what it takes, so far as portrait painting is concerned, I should have thought. He ought to have a London exhibition of his own. That would be the thing to put him on the map."

Beverley laughed and shook her head, as she thought of the times she and Geoffrey had discussed just such an idea in past years.

"Have you any idea what that would cost? Especially for people living in a remote village like this."

"Doesn't his father ever help him?"

"No. He doesn't approve of Geoffrey's way of life at all. He wanted him to go into the business years ago, and I don't think Geoffrey was very tactful in the way he refused. They've been quite bitterly estranged ever since."

"I see." Franklin Lowell narrowed his handsome eyes slightly as he looked ahead. "Have you no good friends?"

"Yes, of course. But no one who could think of putting up so much money. Why should they, come to that?"

"Because he is very talented and you are very nice, I suppose," he replied, with a smile. "I tell you what — I'll give it to you for a wedding present."

"Give me — give us——? I don't understand," gasped Beverley. "What is it you want to give us for a wedding present? — Oh, but you can't anyway. You — you hardly know us."

"Pardon me — I've known you since you were a little girl."

"Oh, but that's different!" She laughed, half touched and wholly charmed.

"On the contrary, it is extremely appropriate. I might even lend my portrait of you for the occasion," he said reflectively. "It's almost essential, I suppose, since it was the cause of bringing us all together, and the basis of my confidence in Revian as an artist. Yes — definitely that will have to have a place in the exhibition."

"But — I simply can't believe it! Do you really mean that you want to — to finance an exhibition of Geoffrey's pictures in a London gallery?"

"Yes. Is it so astonishing? Lots of rich men fancy themselves as patrons of the arts, I believe."

"But — not you," she said, before she could stop herself. Then she coloured and gave him an apologetic little smile.

"Well, no," he agreed, without offence. Indeed, he gave her a wickedly amused glance in return for her smile. "I suppose it isn't much in my line, really. But I do believe in Revian as an artist, and I do like you as a person. And — though I don't know why I should allow myself to be trapped into this sentimental statement — it pleases me to do something towards the future happiness of my little friend in the blue and white dress."

"Oh, Mr. Lowell—" she actually had to swallow a slight lump in her throat — "you really are an awfully nice person, and I don't know how to thank you. Even if Geoffrey doesn't agree——"

"Why shouldn't he agree?"

"Well——" she boggled at the impossibility of putting into words the doubts which assailed her. For had not Geoffrey categorically said that he didn't like Franklin? And, in addition, if there had ever been anything between Sara and Geoffrey, was it quite right that Geoffrey should accept help from the man Sara was to marry?

"You mean," said Franklin Lowell carelessly at this point, "that he doesn't like me and might not want to accept help from me?"

"Why — how did you know?" She was too much taken aback for polite concealment.

"That he doesn't like me?" Her companion was perfectly good-humoured about it. "One always knows, unless one is a fool. I don't much like him either, come to that," he added, without rancour. "But then it isn't necessary that I should."

"Isn't it?" She looked nonplussed. "But why should you help him if you don't like him?"

"I've told you. Because I like you. And I admire his work."

Beverley noted the changed order of his reasons, and wondered just how much value one should set on academic admiration.

"If he were not marrying me, would you make the same offer of help?" she enquired suddenly.

"No. I don't expect so. But don't split hairs about that," he told her carelessly. "Think it over. There is no need to decide anything at the moment. But if you come to the conclusion that you like the idea, it can all be arranged. You can even, if you like, bring in an unknown benefactor, and not tell Revian who is putting up the money."

"I don't think that would be practically possible," she said gravely.

"Anything is practically possible if one wants it sufficiently," he retorted, with a touch of that almost arrogant good humour which is seen only in those to whom success comes naturally. "This is your place, isn't it?"

"Oh — yes." In her eagerness and interest, she had hardly realized that they had arrived in Binwick and were now stopping before her own front door. "Thank you so much for so many things—" she turned and held out her hand to him — "but most of all for this wonderful, unbelievable offer to Geoffrey."

"To you," he corrected, but he smiled.

"Well, thank you, anyway. I hope I haven't taken up too much of your evening."

"No, of course not. I'm not doing anything except drive back home."

"Truly? Then you wouldn't—" she hesitated diffidently — "you wouldn't care to come in and see my mother, would you?"

"If you think she would like me to — of course."

"She would *love* it, I'm sure!" Beverley flushed with pleasure.

"I don't know why she should," he said, with some amusement. But he got out of the car immediately.

"Because when you spend all your time in bed, it's always interesting to see new people," Beverley explained. "Besides — you're a local personality. Rather like someone in a book," she added a little naïvely.

This idea seemed to amuse him too — and very slightly puzzle him. But he followed Beverley up the garden path without any self-consciousness.

When Aunt Ellen opened the door to them, with an expression of half-offended astonishment, Beverley wondered if she had made something of an error in inviting Franklin Lowell in. But, to her amusement — and a good deal to her surprise, he immediately turned on Aunt Ellen such a battery of charm that even she produced a wintry little smile and said she was sure her sister would be happy to see him.

There was, Beverley felt, something strangely exhilarating in the presence of this tall, good-looking, vital creature in their small front room. And when she led the way into her mother's room, she saw reflected in Mrs. Farman's face something of her own rather breathless enjoyment of the impact of Franklin Lowell's personality on their quiet home scene.

He was completely easy in his manner towards her mother, and they liked each other on the instant, Beverley saw. Indeed, after a very few moments, he drew up a chair and sat down, evidently intending to stay for a time, while Beverley curled herself up at the end of the bed a d prepared to enjoy her mother's pleasure in their unusual visitor.

It was surprising how much they found to talk about. But, as a girl, Mrs. Farman had known Elthorpe Hall and its surroundings well.

"I remember old Miss Elthorpe," she said reminiscently. "But she wasn't old Miss Elthorpe then, of course. Only middle-aged and quite extraordinarily difficult. She was supposed to have been crossed in love, which was reckoned to account for all her eccentricities. But I don't know that I believe much in that sort of explanation. It's so easy to blame all one's disagreeable qualities on something in the past, isn't it?"

"Like the psychologists who claim that criminal behaviour in an adult is directly traceable to a well-deserved hiding when one was ten," suggested their visitor.

"Oh, yes!" Mrs. Farman looked at Franklin Lowell with almost affectionate approval. Then, after a pause, she said elliptically, "I think common sense is such a *nice* quality, don't you?"

"It's a wonderful basis for sympathetic understanding," he agreed, with a twinkle. "Has — Beverley—" he hesitated only a second over her name — "told you that I have a picture of her when she was about twelve or thirteen?"

"Yes, indeed! It's Geoffrey's picture of her, isn't it? I'm so glad you have it."

"Why, Mrs. Farman?" he asked rather curiously.

"I'm not quite sure. Except that you would value it for its human, Beverley-ish qualities, and not just make a fuss about it for its artistic merits, I think. Besides, it's nice to think of anything so personal belonging to a friend, rather than a collector."

"You have the most charming way of paying compliments," Franklin told her, with a laugh, as he rose to go. "I hope I may come and see you again."

"Please do. You will always be welcome," Mrs.

Farman said. And then Beverley went with him to the front door.

"Is there anything to be done for her?" he enquired, suddenly much graver than Beverley had seen him before. "She is so charming — and brave."

"I know. Everyone loves her. But — no, I'm afraid there isn't very much. I am sure she liked seeing you, though, and thank you so much for coming in."

"Thank you for asking me," he said. Then he bade her goodbye and went out to his car.

As Beverley turned back into the house again, Aunt Ellen emerged from the kitchen and uttered the first expression of unqualified approval Beverley had ever heard from her.

"Now that," she said, "is what I call a man!" Then she went back into the kitchen again, to see about supper.

CHAPTER SIX

DURING the next few days Beverley lived in a state of painful indecision. She kept on telling herself that few emotional problems are improved by being discussed at length, and that the heart-to-heart talk has accounted for more broken friendships and romances than almost anything else.

But the longing to speak frankly to Geoffrey — to ask him to define his exact attitude towards Sara — was sometimes almost irresistible. To her inmost soul, she longed for some sort of reassurance — some statement from him which might possibly admit a one-time affection but which would also establish beyond all doubt that no feeling for Sara still lingered.

And yet, suppose she did tell him of her doubts and fears, her conjectures and beliefs? If these were groundless, and if he had, in fact, never really returned Sara's love, could anything be more embarrassing or undignified than the position she would then be in?

As for the other possibility — the much stronger probability — that he had indeed at one time loved Sara, what right had she to ask him to admit the fact?

"It isn't even my business if he loved her once but doesn't any longer," Beverley assured herself, with a splendid detachment which reached no further than words. "What's past is past. If it is all over——"

But there, of course, was the rub. *Was* it all over? Or did Geoffrey still hanker after the girl who was divided from him by practical circumstances? Was he, in fact, marrying herself, as second-best, in order to console himself for the loss of the girl he really wanted?

When she was actually with Geoffrey, Beverley was considerably reassured, for his manner to her was as affectionate and intimate as it had always been. It was when she was away from him that she questioned herself in tormenting detail about the real state of affairs. And, during the hours that she sat sewing in her light, pleasant room at the top of Huntingford Grange, there was all too much time to think things over.

Sara made no further reference to their revealing conversation. She remained polite and friendly although, like her mother, not intimate. And she was undoubtedly as pleased as Madeleine with the completed dresses for Lady Welman's charity dance. In addition, like Madeleine, she expressed genuine and friendly interest in the fact that Beverley too was coming to the dance.

She did not ask if Beverley's fiancé would be accompanying her, but she must have passed on the news of the engagement, for Madeleine offered warm congratulations and said she supposed Geoffrey Revian would also be at the dance.

Madeleine was far more expansive than her elder sister. She used to come and talk to Beverley quite a lot — sometimes about Beverley's affairs, as when she enquired about the engagement, but mostly about her own theatrical hopes and aspirations.

"It makes them seem more real when I talk to you about them," she told Beverley. "I always remember the calm way you listened when I first told you I wanted to be an actress, and how you spoke as though anything were possible, if only one were sufficiently determined."

"*Did* I speak like that?" Beverley was amused. "I hope I didn't encourage you unduly in something quite unpractical."

"Oh, no. You merely gave me a new slant on how to look at one's ambitions," Madeleine assured her. "I'm always thinking now of just how I might manage to have at least a year in London at the Academy. I'd *know,* after that, if I were really any good — and I think I'd abide by their decision."

Beverley said nothing, but reflected that few who are once bitten by the urge to act or sing ever accept the discouraging verdict of others. They are always going to give themselves just one more chance and one more year. However, her comments were not necessary. Madeleine ran on quite happily on her own steam.

"Of course," she said, "once Sara is married, with a flat in town, as well as Elthorpe Hall, things will be simpler."

"But is she going to have a flat in town?" Beverley looked up from her work.

"Oh, I expect so. In fact — yes, of course she must! Everyone wants that," Madeleine declared comprehensively. "Besides, think how useful it would be for us all."

Beverley wondered if this view had been presented, in so many words, to Franklin Lowell and, if so, what his reaction had been. But, whether it had or not, Madeleine's casual statement made it increasingly obvious that most of the Wayne family's hopes and plans did indeed depend on Sara's marrying well.

Toni, too, of course, learned very soon of Beverley's engagement, and she rushed into the room on her return from school, still panting from the rapid ascent of two flights of stairs.

"Is it *true*, Miss Farman?" she enquired, with dramatic brevity.

"Is what true?" Beverley looked up and smiled at her.

"Are you really going to marry Geoffrey Revian?"

"Yes. We've known each other for a long time, you know." Beverley explained, in as matter-of-fact a tone as she could, "and now we have decided to get married."

"You aren't wearing a ring." Toni drew near and inspected Beverley's hand a trifle disapprovingly.

"No. He's having his grandmother's ring reset for me. He designed the new setting himself, and it's really lovely."

"Is it?" Toni stood and looked at her, and Beverley guessed that the little girl was busily sorting out some awkward contradictions in her own mind. Then at last she said, "Miss Farman——"

"Yes, Toni?"

"You know what I told you about Sara and Geoffrey Revian, the first day you were here."

"I remember you did tell me something that was worrying you."

"Well, when I told you I saw them with their arms round each other — I guess I was mistaken."

"You mean you *didn't* see them — like that?" Beverley could not quite disguise the eagerness in her voice.

"No, I don't mean that. I did see them, but people do sort of hug each other for other reasons besides being in love, don't they?"

"I suppose they might." Beverley endeavoured to sound as though she were speaking quite academically. "But you also said that Sara was — crying."

"Maybe I was mistaken about that too," said Toni soberly. "Maybe she just had something in her eye."

"That's possible of course," agreed Beverley, hoping that her tone carried more conviction to Toni than it did to herself.

"Anyway, I shall forget all about it now," declared Toni, brightening immensely all at once. "If Geoffrey Revian is going to marry you, there can't be anything between him and Sara, can there? And in that case it's all right for her to marry Franklin, and everyone will be happy."

Oh, blessed simplicity of youthful logic! Beverley wished with all her heart that she could feel the same happy conviction that all was now for the best in this best of all possible worlds. But at least Toni seemed unlikely to indulge in any more worrying on her own account, which was all to the good.

That evening Geoffrey gave her her ring. They had been out together, climbing the beautiful rising moorland slope which lay beyond Binwick, and presently they sat down on the still warm turf, in the soft evening breeze, and looked back on the village, lying below in its sheltered hollow.

It was then that he felt in his pocket, with a slight, conspiratorial smile, and produced the ring in its new setting.

"Oh, Geoffrey—" she leaned over to look at it, so happy in its beauty and reality that almost the last vestige of her fears departed — "how wonderful! It's even lovelier than the sketch suggested."

"It's pretty good," he conceded. "But then it's for a very special person." And, slipping the ring on her finger, he kissed her and said, "Now you're really mine."

"I always was," said Beverley, gravely regarding her ring. And at that he kissed her again and said, "When are we going to be married?"

She had the most absurd impulse to say, "When I am sure that you don't love Sara Wayne better than me." But was this the moment to spoil with unworthy suspicions or suggestions?

He had asked her to marry him. He had given her this beautiful ring in token of the fact. And now he wanted her to choose the very date of their wedding. What sort of cad would she be assuming him to be if she suggested at this point that perhaps he loved someone else?

"Oh, Geoffrey—" she turned and hugged him in a sudden access of hope and confidence — "whenever you say. Except," she added more practically, "that I must finish my work for the Waynes first. They're relying on me, and I couldn't let them down, even for my own wedding."

"Of course not," he agreed, and she wondered if it were only her imagination which made his voice sound rather expressionless. "But is the one situation really dependent on the other?"

"Well — yes. Until Sara's wedding is over" — he sat up suddenly, but she saw he was merely brushing a spider off his sleeve — "I'll be busy on clothes for her and her sisters. After that, I'd like some time to make a few things for myself. Even a dressmaker likes to have a trousseau, you know." And she laughed.

He laughed too — she thought quite gaily, though she could not quite see his face, as he had turned his head and was looking away down the hill.

"I'll put in some intensive work myself, meanwhile," he declared lightly. And then she remembered Franklin Lowell's offer, and she thought this was as good a time as any for mentioning it.

"Geoffrey—" she tried to pick her words carefully — "would this be the right moment for you to have a London exhibition, if that were possible? To show your work — particularly your portrait work — to a larger public, I mean."

"Any moment would be the right moment," he assured her, with a laugh and a shrug. "But you know as well as I do that it isn't a practical possibility. An exhibition, to be successful at all, requires quite a considerable outlay. And I think" — he turned and touched her cheek lightly — "the expenses of getting married must come first."

"But if someone else paid the expenses——?"

"Who else is going to?" He looked puzzled and amused. And then, at something in her expression he was suddenly alert instead of casual. "What do you mean?" There was a sharper, more eager note in his voice.

"Franklin Lowell offered to pay the expenses of a London exhibition of your work, as a wedding present to us both."

"*Lowell* did?" Geoffrey frowned. "You're joking!"

"No, I'm not."

"But why should he make such an offer?" The colour came and went in Geoffrey's face, but whether with excitement or a sort of anger Beverley was not quite sure.

"He said it was because he admires your work and thinks I'm nice," replied Beverley exactly. "He meant it very kindly."

"Nonsense," said Geoffrey. "Men of Lowell's type don't go about doing unrequited acts of kindness. They expect something in return."

"Oh, that's not true!" cried Beverley angrily. "He's truly generous, and I think he *likes* making big gestures."

"Only so that he can pose as a fine fellow, and

feel that other people are under an obligation to him."

"Geoffrey, how can you say such things? There was no suggestion of that at all. And, anyway, why should he want to have you under an obligation to him?"

"I tell you — because it makes him feel a fine fellow," said Geoffrey. But he grinned at her suddenly and seemed to find the whole subject more amusing than annoying, after all. "I must say he has a very fiery champion in you." He pinched the tip of her ear. "I didn't know you were such friends."

"We're not — exactly. At least — he was interested to hear that I was the model for that picture he has. You know — the one of me in the blue and white dress. And, somehow, we got talking, from that point. And he and Sara took me over to Elthorpe to see it again. Then on the way home he asked about our future prospects——"

"With Sara there?" he asked carelessly.

"No, no. We had left her at Huntingford, because she had a bit of a headache and didn't want to drive any further."

"But she knew about our engagement?"

"Yes. I had told them both, while we were still at Elthorpe."

"I see. Go on."

"Well, then he said how much he admired your work, and that he was sure that a London exhibition would put you on the map, so to speak. I explained that this was rather beyond our immediate range, and he made the offer I've told you about.".

"Just like that? out of the blue?"

"Yes. But he did add that there might be some difficulty in making you accept, as he realized you didn't like him," remarked Beverley rather severely.

"He said that?" Geoffrey laughed.

"Yes. But he also said that it didn't matter, because it didn't alter his admiration of your work."

"Or his liking for you?" suggested Geoffrey shrewdly, but he smiled at her.

"He was kind enough to add that," admitted Beverley demurely.

"In fact, the offer was more to please you than to help me?" Geoffrey leaned forward and kissed her. "All right — I don't mind. In fact, I suppose I'd rather have it that way."

"Why?" she asked curiously. But he did not answer her. He just sat there, frowning thoughtfully, and evidently turning over the offer in his mind.

"Geoffrey — you will at least consider it, won't you?" she said pleadingly. "It was so well meant."

"I *am* considering it," he assured her. "Not so much for the noble motives behind the offer as because it is something I've wanted for years. He's right, of course. With reasonable luck, it would alter my whole position." A light of hope and excitement shone in Geoffrey's eyes. A light she had not often seen there, for life had not handed him many of these unexpected chances.

"Oh, darling—" she put out her hand and stroked his arm — "I wish you could have the break you deserve, at last."

"I wish I need not owe the possibility of it to Franklin Lowell," he replied, with a slight face, but he put his hand over hers and pressed her fingers. "Anyway, I shan't look at it that way. I'll consider that I owe the chance to you." He drew her against him and kissed her. "For the offer was made to you — for the very good reason that you're a darling."

She laughed and returned his kiss. This was not the moment to split hairs about the exact reasons which lay behind Franklin Lowell's offer. It was enough that Geoffrey seemed prepared to accept it. And his ring was on her finger.

Beverley looked down at it now, spreading out her fingers, the better to see the sparkle of the stones and the curious and beautiful arrangement of the setting.

"It's the nicest ring anyone ever had," she said.

"Be sure you wear it on Saturday at Lady Welman's dance. I want everyone to know we are engaged," Geoffrey declared.

"But of course! I'll wear it always now," Beverley declared. And although she did not know it, there was something almost defiant in her tone.

Then, as they got up to retrace their steps homewards, she said,

"May I tell Franklin Lowell that the offer is accepted? I think he would like to know."

"Yes. Why not? But—" Geoffrey looked amused again, and just a little curious — "are you in regular contact with him? When are you likely to see him?"

"Oh, I don't know. Perhaps not until the dance. But if I do see him before then, I'd like to be able to say something."

"I leave it to you," Geoffrey told her lightly. "It's between you and him. And, since I'm not a jealous or suspicious sort of fellow, I daresay it's better that way."

She smiled, because she knew that was meant to be a joke. But the words "jealousy" and "suspicion" had too personal a significance for her to find them really amusing.

Beverley had not really expected to see Franklin Lowell before the dance on the Saturday. But on Thursday evening there was a knock at the front door, and when she went to answer it, she found to her surprise that the master of Elthorpe Hall was standing outside with a basket of fruit in one hand and a raffia bag which seemed to contain a couple of plump chickens in the other.

"Hello," he said. "I was passing this way and thought your mother might like these."

"But how kind of you!" Beverley pulled the door open wide. "Do come in, won't you? — or are you in a hurry?"

He was not, it seemed, in a hurry, for he came in immediately. And as Aunt Ellen was standing in the kitchen doorway, somewhat open-mouthed at all this, he said, "May I bring these in?" and marched straight into the kitchen and deposited the fruit and chickens on her well-scrubbed table, much to her consternation.

"Oh, really—" Aunt Ellen fluttered about, flicking non-existent dust off her bright pots and pans — "it isn't very fitting. The kitchen's in such a mess."

This was a palpable misstatement, since everything was always in apple-pie order wherever Aunt Ellen ruled. And, glancing round, Franklin remarked,

"It all looks fine to me. I like a good cottage kitchen." And, sitting down on the side of the table, he swung one leg and smiled at Aunt Ellen, as though he found her young and beautiful.

Now, people often told Aunt Ellen how capable she was and how they didn't know what her sister and niece would do without her. But no one ever looked at her as though she were young and beautiful. And Franklin Lowell's smiling glance had the most extraordinary effect upon her.

She bridled slightly and coloured up, and then she said, in the softest and most friendly tone Beverley had ever heard from her,

"Well, if you like it, you're welcome to stay in it, while I go and see if my sister's awake and ready to see anyone."

"Don't disturb her on my account," Franklin said. But she had already fluttered off, with an air of wanting nothing more than to please the handsome male thing in her kitchen.

To his lasting credit, he made no attempt to exchange a slyly amused smile with Beverley. He merely remarked, "Your aunt is very kind and hospitable."

"Yes," agreed Beverley. And to *her* lasting credit, she did not see fit to add that Aunt Ellen was not always that way.

Instead, she took the opportunity to say, "I spoke to Geoffrey last night about your very kind offer."

"Oh, yes?" He shot her a bright, enquiring glance.

"And, though at first I think he had the feeling that he ought not to accept so much from anyone—" thus did she tactfully recast Geoffrey's early objections — "in the end he was unable to refuse such a wonderful, generous suggestion."

"Good!"

"I can't thank you enough." She held out her hand to him. "*We* can't thank you enough."

"You've done so already," he took her hand and held it lightly in his for a moment. "You're a sweet child. We'll go into details about the whole scheme sometime next week."

"But we aren't being married for some while. There isn't any hurry," she assured him.

"On the contrary, I think it's the kind of present which is best given as soon as it can be arranged," he replied. "If we can turn your Geoffrey into a successful and prosperous portrait painter before your wedding day, so much the better."

She laughed incredulously.

"You make it all sound like something out of a fairy story," she declared. And then Aunt Ellen came back to say that her sister was awake and would be very pleased to see him.

He stayed no longer than ten minutes, since it was obvious that Mrs. Farman had had enough visitors that day already. But, even so, he left behind him the strong impression that an energetic and kindly wind had blown through the house.

"It's to be hoped that girl is good enough for him," was Aunt Ellen's singular comment when he had gone.

"Who? Sara Wayne? She could hardly be prettier or more charming," Beverley declared.

"Looks aren't everything," replied Aunt Ellen, and it was obvious that she had returned to normal.

On Saturday evening, Beverley dressed for the dance with a light heart and a sense of excited anticipation. It was not often that treats of this kind came her way. And, although she had been so busy with dresses for the Wayne girls, she had still found time to make a new dress for herself.

It was of honey-coloured organdie — almost the same shade as her hair — and through it ran a line of shining gold, which caught the light as the skirt spread in billowing folds from an incredibly slender waist-line.

"You look adorable, my darling," her mother declared, when Beverley presented herself for inspection. "If I were a young man, I'd fall in love with you on sight. No wonder Geoffrey wants to marry you."

It was a lovingly prejudiced verdict, Beverley knew, but it put her in the most delicious state of content and did lovely things for her social morale. Then Geoffrey arrived, looking extraordinarily handsome in the unfamiliar grandeur of evening clothes, and his admiration was at least as gratifying as her mother's.

Geoffrey had, in Aunt Ellen's words, "done the thing properly," and they had a hired car to take them to the hideous, but conveniently large mansion where Lady Welman's dance was to take place.

It was — as is usually the case at a charity dance — quite a mixed gathering, but there were few people there whom Beverley knew, and she was pleased to be greeted with something like enthusiasm by the party from Huntingford.

Both the Wayne girls looked breathtakingly lovely in their new dresses and, with a certain amount of innocent pride, Beverley realized that their clothes were commanding almost as much attention as their charming selves. Sara was escorted by Franklin Lowell, of course, and Madeleine was partnered by her brother.

Beverley had not seen much of Andrew Wayne since that first afternoon, when he had driven her from the bus-stop to the house, and she strongly suspected that he could not quite remember who she was. However, he firmly claimed acquaintance with her and evidently had no intention of being regarded as anything but an old friend. A tribute to her appearance which she found both amusing and exhilarating.

It was the most enchanting evening, so far as Beverley was concerned. Geoffrey, with whom she had hardly ever had an opportunity to dance before, proved to be an admirable partner, and she also found herself in demand with several other people, including both Franklin Lowell and Andrew Wayne. In fact, in a modest way, she was a success. A heady and delightful experience against which none of us are proof.

Half-way through the evening she was dancing with Andrew Wayne when he said to her,

"You know, it wasn't until I had a chance to consult Madeleine that I really knew who you were. And I can't tell you how that tantalizing bit of mystery added charm to your presence."

"Thank you." Beverley smiled at him. "I thought you didn't recognize me. I hope the illusion isn't spoiled now you know me."

"On the contrary. I'm now intrigued to know how anyone so decorative can also be clever."

"Clever?"

"Well, you made those gorgeous dresses that my sisters are wearing, didn't you?"

"Oh—that?—yes. I'm a good dressmaker. I don't know that I'd claim more." Beverley laughed.

"But you designed the dresses too, didn't you?"

"In a way—yes. They said what they wanted, and I turned their wishes into practical form."

"You know, you shouldn't be hiding your light under a bushel in a remote village," Andrew Wayne declared earnestly. "You ought to start up on your own in town——"

"Without capital?" She smiled at him and shook her head.

"Well, then, you ought to team up with one of the big fabric firms, in some way." He expertly swung her clear of a couple who seemed to be in some difficulties.

"That's more easily said than done," Beverley told him, but she was aware of a glow of gratification that anyone should rate her work so highly.

"I'm going to speak to my uncle about you," declared Andrew Wayne. "He's on the importing end of the line himself, but he has all sorts of connections. He's always telling me, in a cross sort of way, to prove my initiative and bring him in news of something or someone good in the trade. I'm going to tell him about you."

"No? Really?—are you?" In her surprise and plea-sure, Beverley almost halted, with the result that the clumsy couple, who were still trundling along in the rear, bumped into them, a heavy foot descended on the edge of her dress, and there was a small but ominous sound of tearing.

"Oh, excuse me!"

"No, it was my fault—I stopped——"

"I say—terribly sorry—any damage done?"

There was a flurry of excuses and apology, which dissolved as the couple were swept on again. But Bever-ley knew too much about the construction of her own dress not to realize that some running repairs had probably become necessary.

"I'm afraid I'll have to drop out for a few minutes."

"Why? Did that clumsy oaf tear your dress?" Her partner guided her skilfully to the side of the room.

"Only a few vital gathers at the waist." She laughed philosophically. "But I'll have to go to the dressing-room and catch them up again. Too bad!—the conver-sation was getting extraordinarily interesting."

"We'll continue it later," he assured her. "I remember exactly where we left off."

And then she slipped away upstairs to the improvised dressing-room where a severe but efficient elderly maid of Lady Welman's not only produced the necessary needle and thread, but insisted on doing the repair for her.

"I'm used to a needle and thread, madam," she told Beverley, who refrained from saying that so was she.

"There!" The maid snipped off her thread neatly. "No one will see it now. That's the sort of thing that happens at these *mixed* affairs," she added primly, ap-parently under the impression that no one in good society ever stood on the hem of someone else's dress.

Beverley thanked her and ran downstairs again, meaning to return immediately to the ballroom. But suddenly, through an open doorway, she had the most beautiful glimpse of a moonlit garden. And, irresistibly attracted, she stepped outside, for a breath of the cool night air.

Before her stretched shadowy, tree-lined paths, curiously in contrast to the ugly house behind her. And, with the haunting lilt of a Viennese waltz drifting out from the ballroom, it seemed to Beverley that a nostalgic touch of glamour and charm added magic to the scene.

Almost without thinking what she was doing, she began to follow one of the paths at random, revelling in the delicious freshness of the air after the heat of the ballroom. It was surprising, she thought, that more couples had not found their way out here too.

And then she saw that at least one couple had. For at the end of the path, out of the direct light of the romantic moon, stood two people clasped in each other's arms.

The dress of the girl was unmistakable. Beverley had made it herself, and she could not fail to recognize it as belonging to Sara Wayne.

Well, if Franklin Lowell liked to make love to his fiancée in the garden, who could blame him? The night was sufficiently romantic.

Then the man raised his head, so that she saw him quite clearly for a moment. And it was not Franklin Lowell. It was Geoffrey.

CHAPTER SEVEN

THE shock was so unexpected and so complete that for a moment Beverley really thought her heart had stopped beating.

She felt unable to move. She could not even have said anything, for no words seemed to drift into her curiously empty mind. She could only stand there, staring at the romantic scene which spelled such misery for herself.

Then, suddenly, the fear of being seen in her turn gripped her, and she drew into the shadows, aware that she was trembling and felt slightly sick, that the night was cold and that the music which drifted to her from the ballroom seemed harsh and out of tune.

Without warning and without preparation there had come upon her the complete confirmation of all her doubts and fears. For long enough now she had been chasing shadows, scaring herself with miserable possibilities, comforting herself with cheerful probabilities. And now—in one romantic moonlit glimpse of two figures in a strange garden—she had seen the justification of all her misgivings.

People might, as Toni phrased it, "sort of hug each other for other reasons than being in love." But no two people withdrew to a secluded corner of a garden and embraced for purely social or casually friendly reasons.

Then what, she asked herself, in a sudden fury, did Geoffrey suppose he was doing?

For the first time in her life, blind anger assailed her. How *dared* he make love to her, ask her to marry him, press his ring upon her, suggest that she name a date for their wedding, when all the time he loved Sara Wayne, and took the first opportunity of embracing her?

It was monstrous that these two hollow engagements should go on existing. She would break hers off that very evening—and she would give her reason for doing so. And if Sara's engagement foundered in the wreckage, it was no concern of hers.

In that moment, she was so hurt and furious that she hardly cared who knew the disgraceful truth. She was tired of being hoodwinked. She was tired of seeing Franklin Lowell hoodwinked, come to that. It was time some plain truths were told and they all returned to a decent and truthful set of values.

She found that, while these angry thoughts had been rushing through her mind, she had apparently been walking along one of the cross-paths. She was quite alone now. No one was within sight or sound, and she sat down on a stone bench at the side of the path and buried her face in her hands.

It had been such a lovely evening! and now it was all spoiled. She had been so happy, with her friends and her beloved, in the innocent knowledge that she looked lovely and was admired. And now she felt humiliated and rejected and deceived.

In the immensity of her sorrow and disillusionment she began to sob quietly, and once she had started she could not stop. She forgot about Andrew Wayne, who might well be wondering why she did not return to the ballroom. She forgot that she was in a strange garden, at a well-publicized social gathering, and that she would presently have to make a reasonably good appearance again among strangers. She thought only that her world had fallen to pieces, and that she must weep for its utter dissolution.

And so she went on crying until someone came along the path and paused in astonishment, and Franklin Lowell's voice said,

"For heaven's sake, child! What on earth is the matter?"

"Oh——!" She looked up, startled and dismayed, aware that, though ten minutes ago she had been willing to tell anyone anything, somehow she must conceal from him his own connection with the scene which had so distressed her. Or, at least, that she must do so until she had time for more mature consideration.

"What's the trouble?" He sat down beside her and, without any hesitation, put his arm round her.

It was a strong arm, and an amazingly comforting arm, and as he drew her slightly against him, she realized that she was chilled and that the nearness of someone warm and friendly was soothing.

"Has someone frightened you—upset you?" he enquired, as she still remained obstinately silent, sobbing occasionally like a child and pulling distressedly—and destructively—at the lace corner of her pretty handkerchief.

"Here, don't do that. You'll tear it!" He put his hand over hers and she felt the comforting clasp of his long, strong fingers on hers.

"It's—Geoffrey," she said comprehensively at last, the explanation punctuated by a sharp catch of her breath.

"Geoffrey? What has he been doing? Have you had a quarrel?"

"No."

"What, then?"

"He was k-kissing someone else."

"Oh—I see." She had the feeling that he suppressed a desire to smile, but his tone was completely grave as he said, "Was it a very—important sort of kiss?"

"I think so—yes."

"Not just a regrettable but excusable bit of flirting?"

"No." She shook her head. "You—you remember I told you once that I used to be afraid he was—was fond of someone else. It was—that girl."

"And it wasn't the—what shall I say?—careless salute to a nostalgic page of the past?"

"I don't know what you mean."

"I'm not sure that I do," he confessed. "Only I suppose there are all kinds of kisses, given for all sorts of reasons. Some look very picturesque but don't mean a thing. Perhaps you're distressing yourself quite unduly. After all, he has hardly more than put that very handsome ring on your finger." He lifted her hand and inspected the ring approvingly. "Why would he want to

104

be making serious love to another girl within a few days of doing that?"

"I tell you—he was fond of her before. At least, I'm nearly sure he was. And she was fond of him."

"Then why didn't he marry *her*?"

"He couldn't. There—there was a good reason why they couldn't marry."

"Do you mean she was married already?" He frowned, and it suddenly struck Beverley that, unless she provided a few false details, so shrewd a man as Franklin would not take long to arrive at the truth of the matter. And then what sort of trouble would they all be in?

"Yes," she said hastily, in her panic. "It—it was something like that."

"What do you mean?—it was something like that? Either she is married or she isn't."

"Well, then—she is."

"In other words, he is philandering with a married woman." Franklin Lowell was frowning again. "That's not a very nice situation, I admit."

"It's not—quite like that," Beverley amended hastily, for she was horrified to find she had placed Geoffrey in an even worse light than he deserved. "Perhaps—I'm exaggerating. Perhaps they were—were telling each other that the past was definitely past—that they must really say goodbye to each other and make a fresh start." As she said the words, she realized that they might even fit the true situation as well as the fictitious one she had created.

But Franklin seemed dissatisfied with this explanation.

"I don't know that an embrace was called for, if that was the case," he said dryly.

"They might have been overcome by the—the moonlight and the music and the—the nearness of each other," she suggested, so earnestly that her companion grinned suddenly and said,

"Look here, whose side are you on? I thought I was going to have to explain away your doubts for you. But you're making all the excuses yourself."

She smiled faintly too. But then she drew a long sigh and exclaimed,

"If one could only *know*!"

"Then you must ask him outright. You're entitled to do so, if you saw anything which called so loudly for an explanation."

"I wonder—" she stared almost moodily at Franklin —"I wonder if what I saw was the end of it all, and if I shall spoil everything if I ever let him know that I know about the past."

"I suppose that could be so," he conceded, but doubtfully. "You mean that you want to be generous and give him the benefit of a rather grave doubt?"

"I—think so. I—feel differently now I've talked to you about it. It doesn't seem so—awful, somehow."

"I'm glad, my dear girl, if I've lessened your distress in any way. But——" He rubbed his obstinate chin with a meditative hand, and then obviously thought better of expressing any doubts he might himself entertain.

"Tell me," he said abruptly, "does this girl—this woman—belong to the district?"

"Y-yes."

"Then I'll give you a piece of advice. If Revian has any degree of success with his exhibition, get him away from here. I'm enough of a realist to know that thousands of men have wonderfully happy marriages, even if they start by thinking there's a broken romance in the background. But it's asking for trouble to live anywhere near the pieces."

Beverley laughed faintly and bit her lip.

"It might be difficult to arrange."

"So what?" he shrugged. "Difficulties can usually be overcome. See what the result of his exhibition is."

"You're still willing to—to arrange that, even after what I've told you?" she said anxiously, for it struck her that she might well, in her distress, have blurted out much that was damaging to Geoffrey's prospects.

"My dear child!" Franklin Lowell got up and pulled her gently to her feet. "Revian's social behaviour is no concern of mine whatever. What does concern me is your happiness. Now come along back to the house, and I'll find some side door for you, where you can slip in unnoticed and go upstairs and wash away those tearstains and generally make yourself presentable and gay once more."

"Oh, you're so kind!", exclaimed Beverley. "I don't know what I would have done without you."

"Probably have arrived at the same conclusions on your own," he told her, with cynical kindliness. "But don't look so enchantingly grateful and touching, or I shall probably kiss you in your turn. And then I suppose Sara would somehow come on the scene and draw the wrong conclusions, and the comedy of errors would be complete."

For a wild moment, she felt tempted to say that nothing could more truly represent poetic justice. But she suppressed the impulse and went with him towards the house.

He was as good as his word, and somehow found a deserted side passage into the house. So that she was able to do just what he had suggested—slip upstairs unnoticed and remove all traces of the distressing tears she had shed.

It was a rather grave Beverley who came downstairs for the second time, but no one could have guessed from her general demeanour that less than half an hour ago she had been crying her heart out in the garden.

There are few influences on our behaviour which are stronger than the compulsion to keep up appearances in public. And throughout the rest of that evening Beverley contrived to give an impression of gaiety and lightheartedness which half surprised herself.

The most difficult moment, she knew, would be when she came to the drive home with Geoffrey. How was she to talk to him with any real candour or openness? But equally, how could she erect a barrier of deceit between herself and the one person who meant most to her?

In the end, she hit on a compromise. She would talk of Franklin Lowell's suggestion for their future, but without giving any hint of how she and he had come to discuss this. And Geoffrey himself presented her with the required opening when he said,

"I noticed how well you get on with Lowell. I'm not surprised now that he made you that munificent offer."

"The offer concerns you more personally than me," Beverley pointed out a trifle coolly, "even if he was largely moved by a friendly feeling for me. Which reminds me——he is quite willing to arrange the exhibition as soon as possible, Geoffrey, without waiting for—— for our wedding."

"Is that so?" Geoffrey sounded a little curt. Or perhaps he was just preoccupied.

"Yes. He said——the sooner you were made into a successful and prosperous portrait painter, the better."

Geoffrey laughed slightly.

"That's looking far ahead."

"But one does want to look far ahead at such a time, doesn't one?" she suggested timidly.

"At what time?"

"When one is going to be——married."

"Oh, yes, of course!" Did she detect an odd note of remorse in his tone? "I just didn't get what you meant, for the moment."

"I've been thinking, Geoffrey. Suppose you did make a great success with this exhibition——"

"Dearest girl! let's wait, first, and see what happens. It may be the most almighty flop, however well it's organized.'"

"Yes, I know. And I won't moan if it is," she assured him stoutly. "But Franklin doesn't think it's going to be, and he is a pretty shrewd man of business. He is quite a judge of what the public wants. If it is a success, and you really became in demand, you wouldn't want to go on living here, would you?"

There was quite a long pause. Then Geoffrey said,

"What makes you think that?"

"Well, it wouldn't even be very practical, would it? A man who aspires to paint portraits——"

"I'm not aiming to be a portrait painter only," he interrupted a trifle irritably.

"No. But you're marvellous at that, and it would probably be the really money-making side of your work. Only you can't paint people's portraits if you live in the depths of the country. I suppose we might even have to live in London, mightn't we?"

Again there was quite a pause, while she held her breath.

"We might, I suppose," he said slowly at last. And then, half to himself—"It might be the best way."

"I just wanted you to know that if—if you did decide it was the best way, I wouldn't mind at all."

"What about your mother?" he asked, as they drew up outside Beverley's home.

"I don't know," she confessed. "We should have to make some arrangements so that she was not too far away from us. But one can always get round difficulties. I just want—what is best—for your happiness."

And, in spite of all that had happened that evening— the anger and disillusionment—her voice broke slightly, as she uttered the sad but inescapable truth.

"Oh, Beverley!" He caught her against him suddenly and kissed her on her cheek and on her lips. "You're such a good, darling child. I'm not half good enough for you!"

All the common sense in Beverley—and there was a strong vein of it—told her that it is not a good sign when a man starts saying he is not good enough for a girl. But it was so wonderful to be kissed like that— and to lull one's fears with the idea that perhaps a new beginning had indeed been made that evening—that Beverley was more than half comforted.

She returned his kisses very willingly, and then, bidding him goodnight, ran up the garden path and let herself quietly into the house.

In the most incredible way, life went on quite normally after that.

Beverley had supposed, when she first witnessed that scene in the garden, that all the familiar pattern of existence must surely be disrupted. There must inevitably be a break with Geoffrey—possibly a break between Sara and Franklin. And this, in turn, would presumably put an end to her work at Huntingford Grange (also a prospect to be viewed with dismay) and certainly to any good offices which Andrew Wayne might try to exercise on her behalf with his uncle.

Instead of that, however, the surface of her day-to-day life remained unbroken both at home and at Huntingford. Indeed, plans for Sara's wedding seemed even more definitely taking shape, while the family plans which depended on that event were also more clearly defined when Madeleine blew into the sewing-room early the following week to announce,

"My dear, I've managed it!"

"Managed what?" enquired Beverey smiling, for Madeleine looked so gay and pretty and lively that one smiled instinctively at her.

"I'm going to have my year in London at the Academy of Dramatic Art."

"No?—really?" Beverley was genuinely delighted on her behalf. "Your father has agreed——"

"Not Father—no." Madeleine dismissed her parent's usefulness in this direction with scornful, if good-humoured, emphasis. "I've discussed the whole thing with Franklin. I don't know why I didn't do so before. And he says he is perfectly willing to finance me for an experimental year."

"Is he?" said Beverley soberly, and she found herself wondering if Franklin—shrewd business man though he was—tended to be curiously easily exploited by those he was fond of.

"Have you anything against it?" Madeleine glanced at Beverley in some surprise.

"No, of course not! I—just wondered how you persuaded him. I mean—have you convinced him that you really were sufficiently talented to merit the experiment."

"I didn't," said Madeleine cheerfully. "In fact, he was extraordinarily cynical about any likelihood of my success," she added, without rancour. "But he said that if that was what would really make me happy, he saw no reason why he shouldn't indulge his future sister-in-law to that extent. And he added—which I suppose is true—that it would cost less to keep me as a student for a year in London than to provide me with a mink coat."

"Was he going to give you a mink coat, then?"

"Not that I know of. But rich men *do* give their sisters-in-law that sort of present sometimes, I suppose," replied Madeleine airily.

"I suppose they might," agreed Beverley.

"But you still look disapproving!"

"Not disapproving—no. It isn't my business either to approve or disapprove," replied Beverley very truly. "And I'm very glad for your sake that he feels like making the gesture. It only reminds me that I too have agreed to a very generous gesture. And I hoped he wasn't letting his good heart betray him into *too* much generosity."

"Oh, my dear, he can afford to throw around much more money than that," Madeleine assured Beverley confidently. "But what is he going to do for you?" She looked curious.

"Perhaps he told you. He wants to pay for an exhibition of Geoffrey's paintings in London, as a wedding present to us both."

"Really?" Madeleine was generously delighted on Beverley's behalf. "What a good idea! I've often wondered why anyone so talented as Geoffrey pokes himself away in Binwick, instead of getting out and about among the smart set who really *buy* art, as distinct from admiring it on someone else's wall."

"It's very simple," Beverley said, without offence. "Lack of money."

"But his father's really very well off, isn't he? Revian's is one of the soundest businesses in Castleton. I've heard Father say so often."

"I suppose so. But Geoffrey and his father don't get on together. They haven't for years."

"My goodness, I'd make it my business to get on with *any* sort of parent, if I were the only child of a rich father," observed Madeleine frankly. "So you

111

mean that Geoffrey is more or less a poor man by choice?"

"I suppose you could say so." Beverley smiled slightly. "That was the only way he could pursue the art he loves."

"You have to respect him for it," conceded Madeleine, with an air of recognizing, without being able to understand, some amiable form of insanity. "Who will get all the money when the old man dies?"

"I have no idea."

Madeleine threw up her hands and laughed.

"It's all too, too high-minded for me," she declared. "But possibly that's what preserved Geoffrey safely for you, my child. He's very attractive, and if he'd been rich as well, I can think of one or two people who might have snapped him up." And she looked rather droll, but so entirely without offence that Beverley could smile too and say, with curious sincerity,

"Perhaps it *was* my good fortune that Geoffrey was poor."

During the next week or two she worked hard at Sara's trousseau, while the days grew longer and hotter, and everyone said that this fine weather must break sometime soon.

Geoffrey too was working hard—almost feverishly— to complete one or two unfinished pictures which would add value and importance to any exhibition of his work. He had had a long business talk with Franklin Lowell, in which presumably the two men had successfully camouflaged their dislike of each other, for he had emerged from it in very good humour, to tell Beverley that Franklin Lowell certainly had very handsome ideas about the way he intended to discharge his promise to promote a London exhibition.

"I told you he was genuinely kind and generous," Beverley reminded him.

"Well—all right. But he's a damned lucky fellow too," Geoffrey retorted. "Perhaps that makes it easier to throw largess around. I suppose he has almost every-thing in the world that most people want. Health, wealth, a reasonably interesting job, a fine house—and

112

a beautiful wife. At least he will have that last in a very short time now."

"Then you think anyone who married Sara would be a lucky man?" enquired Beverley, amazed that she suddenly found she could put the question almost casually.

"I suppose so—yes." Geoffrey cast her a quick glance. "She's lovely to look at, and she's a nice girl too. Don't you think so?"

"Yes, of course. But I think there's a hard streak in her."

"Hard?" Geoffrey looked astonished.

"Well—perhaps more hard-headed. I don't think," Beverley said, coolly and deliberately, "that Sara would marry a poor man, just because she loved him, do you?"

There was a second's pause. Then Geoffrey spoke equally coolly.

"No. I suppose you're right there."

"Don't you call that being a little hard?"

"Not necessarily. I think I understand how she feels." Geoffrey spoke slowly. "There are some things one simply cannot give up. With Sara, it's a way of life, I guess, and the desire to put everything right for that family of hers. It's a question of what a thing is worth to you personally. Not unlike the way I felt about breaking with the old man because I just couldn't or wouldn't face life without painting."

"I don't think it's the same thing at all," exclaimed Beverley, with energy. "You sacrificed your comfort and prosperity in order to follow your art. In her case, she sacrificed—I mean we are suggesting she would sacrifice—a worth-while man for the sake of material prosperity."

"Well—" Geoffrey smiled and ruffled her hair, the way he used to when she was a child—"nothing is ever in quite such simple terms as that, I expect. Perhaps the answer is that if a man wanted Sara enough he jolly well ought to make it his business to *be* rich."

He laughed as he said that. But Beverley did not laugh. She merely decided that she would never again discuss Sara with him. For what satisfaction had she extracted from it?

Fortunately, he was so deeply concerned with the arrangements for the proposed exhibition that there was little need to talk of anything else. A suitable gallery had now been selected, a date had been fixed in the early autumn, when people would be returning to town after the holidays, and a certain amount of what Franklin called "indirect publicity" was already in hand.

To Beverley it seemed that Geoffrey had never been more deeply absorbed in his work, nor more eagerly optimistic about the future. The mood of confidence was even reflected in his work and, partial though she was, Beverley knew it was true that he was doing some of the best painting he had ever done.

Insensibly her own optimism and confidence deepened, and she began to dare to hope that the unhappy infatuation for Sara—the existence of which she could no longer doubt—might perhaps die a natural death, in the glow of a long-delayed artistic success.

Almost every evening she would go down to the studio and watch him work—almost as she had in the days when she was a child—and, to her infinite pleasure he started a portrait of herself, declaring that he must have her in the exhibition, if only as his mascot.

"Franklin is going to lend you the one in the blue and white dress, in any case," she told him. But she was happy that he should want one of her as she was, in addition.

He worked with extraordinary rapidity, as though the sureness of his hand simply could not fail him, where she was concerned, and as she saw the portrait taking shape beneath his hand, she knew it was the best thing he had ever done.

Within a matter of days all the main work of the painting had been accomplished, and when Beverley strolled down the village street, one bright July evening, she guessed that he would finish the work either that evening or the next day.

She felt happy about it—and she felt happy about him. Much happier than she had done for a long time.

For in painting her picture he had seemed, in some strange way, to grow nearer to her again, and, as he did so, to achieve a certain inner tranquility which—she realized now—had been missing for a long time.

Beverley was all the more distressed, therefore, to find him almost on the doorstep, ready to go out although he must have been expecting her. And she saw immediately, from his almost agitated expression, that something was wrong.

"Oh, Geoffrey, what is it?" She tried to keep the alarm out of her tone and failed.

"Something has happened——" his voice was even a little hoarse.

"Not about the exhibition? Nothing has gone wrong about that?" she cried anxiously.

"The exhibition? No, no—that's all right. It's my father," he said, and he passed a slightly bewildered hand over his face. "He's had a bad heart attack, and they don't expect him to live the night. And he's asked for me, Beverley. After all these years—he's asked for me."

CHAPTER EIGHT

"YOUR father?—Oh, Geoffrey, I am sorry." In that first moment, she thought only of his distress. "I won't keep you. You must go at once, of course."

"Walk up the street with me." He slipped his hand round her arm and pressed it, as though he found some sort of reassurance from the contact with her.

"Yes, of course. Are you going to take the bus into Castleton?"

"No. I'm hoping Barton will have the village taxi free. I was going up to enquire when you arrived."

They walked up the village street together, and she tried to think of something comforting to say, for she saw he was badly in need of some sympathy and support.

Until then, she had never thought of there being any bond between Geoffrey and his father. The disagreement between them had been so deep, and its existence so long, that it had not occurred to her that, even in an emergency, either of them could feel differently. But blood, she realized now, is a strange thing. It was obvious that Geoffrey was deeply moved by what had happened.

"I'm glad he asked for you," she said at last. "It shows he was really fond of you—in spite of everything."

"Yes. Yes, that's what I thought. It makes me feel—rather awful now. As though I ought to have found some way of bridging the gap before."

"But you did try, didn't you?"

"Not very persistently." Geoffrey shook his head and looked even more unhappy. "I was always afraid of appearing to be after his money."

"Well, I suppose some pretty hard things were said between you, and—one does have one's pride," Beverley said.

"That's what I told myself. But then—something like this happens, and you wonder what pride matters, beside the fact that the old man was lonely and obstinate, and quite incapable of making the first move."

"He has made the first move now," Beverley pointed out.

"I know. And that only goes to show how much he must really have wanted us to get together again. I could kick myself."

"Don't be too harsh on yourself." She pressed his hand against her. "It's difficult to see things in their right proportion at a time like this. Just get there as quickly as you can, and try to make him understand that you want to be friends as much as he does."

This was a poor sort of consolation, Beverley knew, but it was the best one could do with words. And just then they arrived at what was known in the village as "Barton the taxi"—a composite term which included Mr. Barton himself, his small house, garage and large car of ancient vintage.

Fortunately Barton the taxi was disengaged, and only too pleased to drive Geoffrey into Castleton, especially when he heard the address to which they were to go. His prominent, red ears positively quivered with interest, as though tuning themselves in to some dramatic story which would inevitably be unfolded.

"You wouldn't come too?" Geoffrey caught Beverley by the hand again, just as she was about to say goodbye to him.

"Willingly, if I thought I could be of any use," she said. "But I don't think your father wants to see anyone but you just now, Geoffrey. This evening belongs to him alone."

"Yes, of course. You're right." He kissed her hard.

"But if for any reason you want me later, just send Barton back for me."

"Very well."

Then Geoffrey got in beside Mr. Barton, and, with a certain amount of bucking and spitting, the taxi drove off.

Beverley slowly retraced her steps homeward, reflecting soberly, as she went, on the great amount of family unhappiness which could be avoided if only obstinacy and pride were not such common human failings.

"You're back early," observed Aunt Ellen as she re-entered the cottage. "Is something wrong?"

This would have been Aunt Ellen's automatic suggestion, whatever Beverley's reason for returning early, and it was slightly annoying to have to admit that, on this occasion at any rate, Aunt Ellen was right.

Beverley therefore merely said briefly, "Geoffrey had to go and see his father," and went into her mother's room.

Aunt Ellen, however, knew at least as much about the private affairs of most people in Binwick as they knew themselves—and sometimes more. So she immediately assessed the momentous quality of this simple statement.

"See his father?" She followed Beverley. "Geoffrey has gone to see his father?—Did you hear that?" She skilfully drew her sister into the circle of interesting news and discussion. "Geoffrey has gone to see his father, and, to my certain knowledge, they haven't spoken for years. Why should he go now?"

"His father sent for him." Beverley sat down by her mother's bed and ran her hands through her fair hair. "He is very ill—it seems he had a heart attack and may not live long—and he wanted to see Geoffrey."

"That means he is going to do something about his will," declared Aunt Ellen, divided between the rival attractions of having Geoffrey cut off with a shilling or her niece's fiancé endowed with a fortune. Characteristic pessimism, however, triumphed over even family feeling, and after a moment she added, "He was always a hard man, Peter Revian. He's going to tell Geoffrey that he's leaving it all to charity, you mark my words."

"I think he just wanted to make sure that he saw Geoffrey again," Beverley replied simply. "They must have been—closer than I ever supposed. At least, at one time they must have been. I don't think I have ever seen Geoffrey more moved or distressed."

"Well, the situation *is* moving," her mother said thoughtfully. "And particularly it's sad to think how much time has been wasted when they could have been friends again."

"That's what I feel, Mother. But—you can't be wise for other people."

"It's difficult enough to be wise for oneself," remarked Aunt Ellen—a sober truth which no one could dispute. "Have you thought how this may affect you, Beverley?"

"Me?" Beverley looked startled. "How do you mean?"

"Well, if there is some sort of reconciliation, and old Revian leaves Geoffrey everything, he'll be a rich man instead of a poor one."

"I—suppose he would be—yes," Beverley agreed slowly. "I hadn't thought of that."

"You're too unworldly," Aunt Ellen told her.

"No, she isn't," declared Beverley's mother. "She merely thought first of the human side of things, which was quite right. But—it is a fact, dear, as Ellen says— this could make a great difference to you and Geoffrey. Your prospects could be infinitely brighter."

"You don't know," countered Aunt Ellen cautiously. "Perhaps only *his* prospects will be brightened. Geoffrey might decide he wanted someone else, more socially desirable, if he found himself a rich man."

Beverley stared at her aunt, indescribably shaken at having her inmost fears so unexpectedly put into words, even though it was no more than natural for her aunt to prophesy thus. But Mrs. Farman cried impatiently,

"Oh, Ellen, you do have the most uncomfortable and ridiculous ideas! Why should Geoffrey want someone else, for heaven's sake? He has been in love with Beverley for years."

"Well—perhaps you're right." Aunt Ellen seemed impressed by her sister's vehemence, even to the extent of admitting a glimmer of light into the general gloom of her prognostications. "But one never knows," she reiterated, on principle.

Still Beverley said nothing. She managed to smile

slightly, as though associating herself with her mother's protest while not really taking Aunt Ellen seriously. But she was aware of a terrible chill at her heart. For, absurd though Aunt Ellen's suggestion might be, as a general view, there was still the particular aspect, about which her aunt and her mother knew nothing.

If, in fact, Geoffrey did suddenly find himself a rich man, how was that likely to affect the situation between him and Sara Wayne?

The rest of the evening dragged slowly by. But, although Beverley stayed up later than usual—and the light in the front-room window advertised the fact— there was still no news of Geoffrey when she finally went to bed, not long before midnight.

It was Saturday the following day, which meant that Beverley did not go to Huntingford Grange, and was, therefore, at least available for any news as soon as it came.

Thanks to the village grapevine (as represented by the milkman and the postman) Aunt Ellen was able to report that Geoffrey had stayed in Castleton for the night, and that Barton the taxi had returned quite early the previous evening, with the news that old Mr. Revian was supposed to have rallied a little.

"How did Barton know that?" enquired Beverley curiously.

"I suppose he asked someone at the house how the old man was," replied Aunt Ellen, with a simple understanding of how these things were done. "But that would be early in the evening, of course. It's around midnight and the early hours that old people are at their lowest."

It was obvious that, so far as she was concerned, Mr. Revian was already prepared for his funeral, and when Geoffrey arrived at last, about eleven o'clock, she automatically composed her features into an expression of condolence.

Geoffrey, however—who arrived in a chauffeur-driven Rolls-Royce, instead of in Barton the taxi— looked almost eager, and certainly a good deal happier than when Beverley had last seen him. And he came in with an air of briskness and optimism much at variance with Aunt Ellen's muted gloom.

"Oh, Geoffrey—he's better, isn't he?" exclaimed Beverley, as soon as she saw him. "You look quite different."

"Do I?" Geoffrey smiled and kissed her. "Well, I *feel* different. I can't tell you how different! It's true that the old man is quite a bit better, though not by any means out of the wood yet. But—oh, darling—" he hugged her so tightly that she gasped and laughed—"in some extraordinary way, everything is all right between us again."

"Everything?"

"Well—we haven't talked of absolutely everything, of course," he admitted. "Only the old bitterness and misunderstanding seem quite gone. He's much—gentler and more tolerant. I felt like a boy again! And it made me remember things I'd forgotten for years."

"What things?" She stood smiling at him, indescribably happy in his new happiness.

"How we were good friends in the school holidays," Geoffrey said slowly. "And he used to show off a bit to his friends because I could draw and paint better than their kids could. Oh—it all sounds rather silly and trivial, but such a lot of one's early life is made up of such things, I suppose."

"But of course! And a lot of any parent's happiness is made up of such things, too, I imagine."

"I guess so. He was so happy to talk of old times." Geoffrey smiled again, as though recalling something that had pleased him immensely. "He isn't allowed to talk much at a time, of course. But I think it did him good to have me recall things. And now, Beverley, he wants to see you."

"To see me?" She was a little taken aback. "Does he?"

"Well, of course. I told him I was engaged to be married, and he was delighted and said he must see you for himself before—well, anyway," Geoffrey amended hastily, "he naturally wants to see the girl I'm going to marry."

"How—nice." She smiled slowly, and she felt a warmth in her heart where there had been a chill ever since Aunt Ellen's words of the previous evening. For, somehow, the idea that Geoffrey's father wanted to see her—and, even more, that Geoffrey had spoken so positively of her as the girl he was going to marry—carried more reassurance with it than even his actual proposal had done.

"When does he want me to come?" she asked.

"Now. Or, at least, as soon as you can," Geoffrey explained. "He was resting when I left, but he said he hoped to see you during the day. I thought that, if you could come back with me now, you'd be available whenever he did feel like seeing a visitor."

"Yes, of course. Sit down, Geoffrey, and Aunt Ellen will bring you some coffee. I won't be more than a few minutes getting ready."

Beverley went first into her mother's room and explained briefly what had happened, and then went to her own room to change into something suitable for a visit to one's future father-in-law.

Here Aunt Ellen came to her—having supplied Geoffrey with her invariably excellent coffee.

"So you're going to meet Geoffrey's father at last?" She was agog at the news. "It will be an important meeting, Beverley. You want to make a good impression, if you're not to undo all the good this reconciliation has done."

"I hope to make a good impression," replied Beverley a trifle dryly, as she slipped out of her morning-dress, and opened the wardrobe to consider what she would wear.

"Something quiet, dear," urged Aunt Ellen behind her. "In keeping with the seriousness of the situation. But not black. That always seems so—previous, as one might say."

"I don't intend to wear black," Beverley assured her. "I shall wear my grey dress, with the white collar and cuffs."

"Grey?" Aunt Ellen shook her head doubtfully.

"Half-mourning, you know. Doesn't it look a little—well——?"

"No, it doesn't," retorted Beverley firmly. But, almost hypnotized by Aunt Ellen's views on decorum in dress, she added a scarlet belt which could in no way be classed as half-mourning.

"That's better," declared her aunt, in as nearly a satisfied tone as she ever produced. And Beverley went downstairs again, ready to accompany Geoffrey.

It seemed strange to step into a sumptuous car with Geoffrey, and to have a respectful chauffeur calling him "Sir" and evidently regarding him as an important person. For so long Geoffrey had been the slightly bohemian, easy-going figure in her life. Now he was, willy-nilly, being invested with a sort of dignity and importance which made him seem a little like someone else.

It was nearly an hour's drive into Castleton, and Geoffrey had plenty of time to tell her more of the meeting between his father and himself. How the estrangement of years had melted in the warmth of a real reconciliation, and how his father had even gone so far as to ask with some eagerness about his progress in the world of art. A subject which, in the old days, had been absolutely taboo.

"I told him about the exhibition Franklin Lowell is arranging," Geoffrey recalled with a smile. "And he seemed quite annoyed that anyone else should do something for me. He said something to the effect that there was no need for Lowell to interfere, and that he would 'see to all that' himself."

"But we couldn't be so ungracious as to fling back Franklin's offer at him now," protested Beverley anxiously.

"No, no, of course not." Geoffrey brushed that off easily. "There is always a way of explaining these things. What is important is that the old man showed clearly that *he* wanted to give me any support that is necessary. And if he recovers——"

Geoffrey stopped for a moment, and Beverley quickly put a reassuring hand over his.

"He may well recover, my dear. He has already rallied so well."

"Yes—I know. I keep on telling myself that. And there's much more will to live in him, now that things are all right between us."

"Of course."

"If he recovers," repeated Geoffrey, more confidently this time, "I think he means to take an active interest in whatever I am doing. And if I really pulled off a successful show of my pictures, he is in the mood to lap the whole thing up and enjoy it as much as myself."

Beverley smiled and said he could hardly ask more.

"It's difficult to take in how everything has changed—in a matter of hours." Geoffrey passed his hand over his face, as though brushing off something which had obscured his vision until now. "This time yesterday, all the horizons were limited. And now—" he laughed and gave himself a little shake—"I'm only just beginning to take in what this could mean."

She said nothing. She wondered in just what terms he saw his horizons widening, and if Sara Wayne had suddenly entered the picture of the unexpected future that stretched before him. But there was no possibility of finding out anything about that, and, in any case, they arrived just then at their destination.

The chauffeur hurried round and opened the door of the car, and Beverley stepped out and stood for a moment regarding the solid, handsome house which had once been Geoffrey's home. There was a slightly old-fashioned air about it, but there was no doubting that it was the home of very prosperous people.

Again it was incongruous to imagine Geoffrey in connection with this place, just as it had been to see him at ease in the luxurious car. And, as Beverley entered the house, she was aware of a sort of nervousness mingling with her natural interest.

"Come, darling——" Geoffrey led her into what she took to be a morning-room, which was furnished in a pleasant, if rather solid style. And here, a good deal to her surprise, she was presented to a handsome, but severe-looking lady with grey hair.

"This is my aunt, Mrs. Mercer," Geoffrey explained, and Beverley found herself being greeted politely rather than cordially.

With difficulty, she bit back the exclamation, "I never even knew you *had* an aunt!" And suddenly she thought how little she really knew of Geoffrey's family background, in spite of all the years they had been friends.

In those early days, the whole subject of the family estrangement had been too painful for her to ask many questions, and, although Geoffrey had poured out his hopes and fears to her, somehow he had never given her a clear picture of the home and family he had left.

Now, in some strange way, he seemed to be slipping back into a scene which to her was quite alien, and in this unfamiliar scene even he seemed unfamiliar.

With an effort, Beverley controlled her rising nervousness, and while Geoffrey went to see if his father were ready to receive them, she made what conversation was possible with a complete stranger who showed no special wish for them to become any better acquainted.

It is difficult, of course, to assess the wheels within wheels which exist in any family. But Beverley thought it not improbable that Mrs. Mercer had been the most important person in her brother's life during recent years, in which case she was not particularly likely to welcome anyone else—either her nephew or his fiancée —if she thought they might upset an arrangement which was to her own advantage.

The exchange of civilities was becoming rather uphill work by the time Geoffrey reurned, with the news that his father was awake and ready to receive Beverley.

"It won't be more than a short visit," he explained, "because he tires easily. But he is very anxious to meet you, Beverley."

Together they went up the wide, handsome staircase to a room with double doors. Geoffrey knocked softly, and a nurse in a stiffly starched uniform admitted them.

It was a large room, handsomely furnished but curiously impersonal. There was nothing impersonal, however, about the grey-haired man propped up in the bed. Ill though he obviously was, he dominated the scene, and the penetrating glance which he directed upon Beverley as she crossed the room missed absolutely nothing about her, she felt sure.

In some indefinable way, he was extraordinarily like Geoffrey. But a far more decided, clearly drawn version of Geoffrey. The family resemblance was unmistakable, but the difference in temperament was unmistakable too.

"So you're the girl Geoffrey is going to marry?" He took Beverley's hand and looked at her searchingly.

"Yes, Mr. Revian," Beverley said.

"Well, you're pretty enough." That was a plain statement rather than a compliment, she saw.

Beverley smiled.

"He knows prettier girls than I am," she assured Geoffrey's father. "I don't think that's his principal reason for wanting to marry me."

"No?" The man in the bed smiled too then. "What is, then?"

"I don't know. You would have to ask Geoffrey that. I only know my own reason for wanting to marry him."

"And that is——?"

"That I love him," Beverley said simply. At which Geoffrey came and put his arm round her.

"She looks a good child," the old man said to his son. And then, to Beverley—"So you think you can manage my boy?"

"As much as anyone should be managed by another person," Beverley conceded, again with a smile.

"Hm—he's difficult, you know. He's my son, so he is almost bound to be," he added, with pride rather than regret, Beverley thought.

"We're all difficult, Mr. Revian, until someone finds the key to us," Beverley replied gravely.

"Quite a student of human nature, eh?" he said, but not unkindly. "Who are your people?"

"No one very special," Beverley told him, without embarrassment. Then she explained briefly about her father and mother, and old Mr. Revian frowned thoughtfully.

"Then your grandfather must have been Angus Trenton?"

"Yes, he was."

"I remember him when he was Vicar of St. Stephen-in-the-Woods. Best man in the pulpit that I ever heard, and a grand worker in the parish too. If you have half his good sense and character, you'll do very well for my boy. Better than anyone with a fancy name and not much between the ears."

"Oh, thank you!" Beverley smiled and blushed. "I won't make any special claims, on the strength of being the granddaughter of Angus Trenton. But I will do my best to be a good wife to Geoffrey, on my own account."

"No one can promise more," replied the man in the bed, and raising his hand, he patted her cheek. "You'll have to go now." His hand fell back slackly on the counterpane, as though even that slight effort had been too much for him. "I tire easily. But I'm glad to have seen you. And I hope to see you again.—Who knows——?"

But he shut his eyes after that. And, with a light touch on his hand, which was half a goodbye, and half a caress, Beverley turned away.

Geoffrey accompanied her out of the room and down the stairs once more. And, on the way, he put his arm round her and gave her an approving hug.

"He liked you, Beverley!"

"I liked him," she replied simply. "I—I hope there will be many opportunities of knowing him better."

"Well—" Geoffrey sighed—"at least he is holding his own, at the moment. Come and have some lunch now. And perhaps later——"

"Oh—do you think I should stay to lunch?" Beverley said doubtfully, as she remembered the lack of warmth in Mrs. Mercer's manner.

"Why, of course. Why not?" Geoffrey looked surprised.

"I didn't want to appear to—to make myself at home here, when I'm quite a stranger as yet. I thought——"

But Geoffrey would have none of that. So Beverley stayed to lunch—a well-served and admirably cooked meal—and again made what contribution she could towards some uninspired and very formal conversation.

Geoffrey had seemed to think she might be asked for again by his father. But when, early in the afternoon, the nurse reported that her patient was asleep and would certainly not be seeing anyone else that day, Beverley said that she must go home.

"You stay here, Geoffrey. Your place is here," she told him. "But I have stayed as long as I should, and, anyway, Mother will be expecting me back. I ought to catch the three-thirty bus."

"What's the matter with the car?" he asked rather impatiently.

"Your aunt said something about going out this afternoon," Beverley reminded him. "I'm sure she will need the car, and frankly I would rather go by bus than ask her to make any re-arrangements. I've been going by bus all my life—" she smiled at him mischievously— "so there's no need to look on it as a hardship now."

"All right." He smiled too then. "I'll walk down to the bus-stop with you."

He seemed to be feeling the need for her presence, and it touched her and pleased her immensely that this was so. Not since the old, happy days before Sara Wayne had come into her life, had she felt so truly necessary to him, so much a part of his plans.

Undoubtedly his father's expressed approval had something to do with this—if only because it made him see his marriage as something which fitted perfectly into the new pattern of life which was opening for him. But, in addition, there was this eager, half-boyish dependence on her in trouble which was touchingly and deliciously reminiscent of the old days.

As they stood waiting for the bus, he unselfconsciously held her hand in his. And when it arrived and she turned to say goodbye to him, he kissed her hard and said,

"Thank you, my darling, for all your support."

She kissed him in reply and climbed into the overcrowded bus, hardly noticing that anyone else was there, or that she was going to have to stand in discomfort among a shopping-laden crowd, at least for part of the way.

What did a little thing like that matter beside the fact that Geoffrey loved her and needed her? That his father approved of her and had virtually set his seal on the marriage. How small and unnecessary her fears and anxieties of the last few weeks now seemed. She had tormented herself for nothing.

There were two or three other stops before the bus actually left Castleton, and gradually the number of passengers thinned, until Beverley found herself a seat near the front, where she seemed likely to sit in happy solitude.

At the last stop in the town, however, a few more people joined the bus, and one of them came running to the front to drop into the seat beside Beverley.

"Hello, Miss Farman," said Toni's clear and rather penetrating voice, "what are *you* doing in Castleton on a Saturday afternoon?"

"I might ask you the same thing." Beverley turned to smile at her, for she was fond of the youngest Wayne. "You don't go to school on Saturday, do you?"

"I should think *not!*" Toni dismissed such a gruesome idea with emphasis. "I've been to spend the morning with Wendy Tulley, and they asked me to lunch, and was I glad!"

"Really?" Beverley was amused. "Was it such a good lunch, then?"

"Oh, it was all right, you know." Gastronomic niceties did not find a place in Toni's interests yet, it was evident. "But it wasn't that. I was glad not to be at home today, because something perfectly awful has happened, Miss Farman."

"Has it?" Beverley remained magnificently calm before this tragic announcement, because she had had previous experience of the things which ranked as disasters in Toni's estimation. "What is it?"

"I don't know that I'm supposed to tell anyone." Toni dropped her voice and glanced round the bus. "But I guess it doesn't matter telling you, because in a way you're almost family. And, anyway everyone will have to know soon. Sara has broken off her engagement, Miss Farman. And you simply can't guess what a to-do there is about it."

CHAPTER NINE

"SARA—your sister—has broken off her engagement?" repeated Beverley in utter consternation. "You mean— she isn't going to marry Franklin Lowell?"

"No." Toni shook her head emphatically. "She just isn't going to marry him at all."

She spoke as though there were degrees of marriage and Sara had rejected them all.

"But—how perfectly awful!" Beverley felt a dreadful sinking sensation which was almost physical somewhere in the region of her heart. "You—you can't have got it right, Toni. There must be a mistake. Perhaps they have had a misunderstanding of some sort. Something that——"

"Oh, no. There's no misunderstanding about it," Toni declared. "Sara told us all at breakfast-time this morning. Mother went quite white and Father nearly choked, and Madeleine said what about her year at the Academy of Dramatic Art? which I thought rather selfish of her."

"And what," asked Beverley in a fascinated tone, "did you say?"

"I said what about Franklin? But no one took any notice," Toni explained, "because I suppose they were all thinking about themselves."

"I suppose—they were," agreed Beverley slowly. And, unexpectedly, she bent and kissed the little girl's cheek. "You're a good child."

"Why?" enquired Toni, to whom this view was evidently novel.

"Oh—never mind. It would take too long to explain. But I—I'm very sorry to hear about this, Toni."

She could not say that she was shocked and frightened beyond description, or that the very foundations of her new-found security and happiness were rocking. She could only say conventionally that she was sorry to hear the news. And then add, with unconvincing optimism,

"But perhaps it will all blow over. Perhaps Mr. Lowell will be able to talk her out of this idea."

"No." Toni shook her head again. "I think he'd already said all he had to say last night. They must have settled it then, because they were out together. And this morning she came to the breakfast-table without her ring."

"I see."

The bus jogged on over the rough country roads, and Beverley stared ahead and tried to tell herself that there was no need to panic. Even if Sara had decided that she could not marry Franklin Lowell, after all, this did not necessarily mean that she hoped to marry Geoffrey.

"It isn't even as though she could possibly have known about his changed prospects," thought Beverley. "At least——" She felt her heart miss a beat.

Could Sara possibly have known?—and was that anything to do with her sudden decision not to go on with her engagement to Franklin?

Beverley did some feverish calculation, and decided that unless Geoffrey had deliberately telephoned his news to Sara, there could be no possibility of her having known the changed circumstances.

"And he wouldn't do that," Beverley assured herself. "Why should he? Besides—there was nothing in his manner to suggest that he had even thought of Sara since he had the news about his father."

"Why were you in Castleton, Miss Farman?" asked Toni again, at this moment, in innocent curiosity. "Were you just shopping?"

"No." Beverley roused herself from her thoughts with an effort, and decided there was no harm in telling the exact truth. "Geoffrey's father was ill, and sent for him. And then he decided that he would like to see me too. I've just come from his place now."

"Geoffrey Revian's father?" Toni looked interested. "But I thought they weren't on speaking terms."

"Well, they are now," Beverley said briefly.

"D'you mean there's been a reconciliation?" enquired Toni, scenting drama.

"You might call it that, I suppose."

"Was it a *deathbed* reconciliation?" Toni evidently liked that idea immensely.

"No. I hope Mr. Revian is going to get well."

"But he might not?" suggested Toni, in the interests of dramatic possibilities which, for the moment, outweighed even her characteristic kindliness.

"He is very ill," Beverley conceded. And, because she could not resist trying this line of enquiry, she added casually, "Had you not heard anything about it?"

"No. How should I?" Toni looked surprised.

"Oh, well—Mr. Revian is a very well-known man in the district. I thought perhaps—perhaps one of the family might have heard something."

"If so, no one told *me*." Toni sounded slightly aggrieved. "No one ever does tell me anything."

"Well, I've told you something now." Beverley smiled slightly.

"Yes. Thank you *very* much, Miss Farman," Toni said gratefully. "I'll like telling the others. And I can really say that Geoffrey is reconciled with his father?—and that you've seen him?—and that he liked you?"

"Yes. I think you can say all that," Beverley told her slowly, for there seemed no point in delaying the news. "But how do you know that he liked me?"

"He couldn't help it," said Toni simply. At which Beverley felt oddly cheered.

Presently they began to near the stop for Huntingford Grange, and suddenly Toni said,

"Why don't you get out with me, Miss Farman, and call in at home? You might cheer them up a bit."

"I don't think I can flatter myself that I should do that." Beverley smiled and shook her head. But she was immediately assailed by the most terrible temptation to hear for herself what had really happened, and to see the effect of her own news.

"You would, you know," Toni told her. "They all like you. And by now they must be tired of talking to one another about this business."

"But I have no possible excuse for coming." Beverley was weakening, in spite of her better judgment. "It

133

would look as though I were just—just drawn there by curiosity, which would be unpardonable."

"You could call in for some work you had forgotten," suggested Toni practically.

"I—well, yes, I suppose I could do that." Beverley felt her resistance crumbling, and she snatched at the proffered excuse. "Yes, as a matter of fact, there *is* something I would rather like to take home with me. There is so little time——"

And then she stopped. Because, of course, if Sara were not going to marry Franklin Lowell, after all, there was all the time in the world.

"There's no great rush now," agreed Toni soberly. "But do come, just the same."

So Beverley got off the bus when Toni did, and together they walked up the lane to Huntingford Grange.

Fortunately she was saved from making her own excuses, for Mrs. Wayne was in the hall when they entered, and Toni immediately broke into explanations.

"Oh, Mother, I met Miss Farman on the bus, coming back from Castleton, and she's called in to fetch some work she forgot to take yesterday. And she's been into Castleton to see Geoffrey Revian's father, who is very ill and just been reconciled to Geoffrey, in case he dies. Isn't that interesting?"

"Very interesting," said Mrs. Wayne absently. "Good afternoon, Miss Farman. Do come upstairs. I—I should like to speak to you."

For the first time in Beverley's experience, Mrs. Wayne seemed uncertain in her manner, and Beverley found it in her heart to be genuinely sorry for the mother of the beautiful but unpredictable Wayne girls. Her scale of values might be very worldly, but in her way she wanted what she thought was best for her daughters. It must, Beverley supposed, seem to her that Sara had gone out of her mind.

Together they mounted the stairs to the sewing-room, meeting no one else on the way. And, once they were there, Mrs. Wayne shut the door and said—with a dramatic simplicity worthy of Toni herself,

"Miss Farman, Sara has broken off her engagement."

"Yes—I'm terribly sorry. As a matter of fact, Toni did tell me just the salient fact," admitted Beverley. "But is it absolutely final, Mrs. Wayne? I mean, many girls do have last-minute doubts or a feeling that——"

"She says she won't even discuss it."

"Does she give any reason for her decision?"

"Only that she simply doesn't want to marry him, after all." Mrs. Wayne raised her hands and let them fall again, in a gesture of helplessness. "I don't understand her. He is kind, he's rich, he's a very decent fellow, and he is much the best match in the county. What *does* she want?"

"Perhaps," suggested Beverley, unable to keep back the words, "she wants someone else."

"Someone else, Miss Farman? But who else could she want? There is no one in our circle even comparable with Franklin, from the point of view of marriage."

"She might," Beverley said doggedly, "have found she is really in love with someone else. Someone not specially suitable, perhaps, but someone that *she* wants. These things do happen. Has she never given any—any indication of such a thing?"

"No. Of course not." Mrs. Wayne looked as though Beverley had suddenly broken into a foreign language which was not very familiar to her. "She has been engaged to Franklin for months. Elthorpe Hall has been renovated to suit her wishes. More than half her trousseau is made, as you yourself know. How could she suddenly find that she wanted someone else?"

"Perhaps—" again Beverley spoke rather as though she could not help it—"perhaps it was not so sudden."

"I don't understand you."

"Oh—it was just an idea——" All at once, Beverley was frightened at the way she had let the conversation get out of hand, in her irresistible desire to put her own doubts to the test.

"Do you mean," said Mrs. Wayne slowly, "that she might have been fond of someone *before* Franklin came along?"

"It's—possible, isn't it?"

"But I think she would have told me."

Beverley was silent, surprised that Mrs. Wayne could know so little about her own child. For if ever anyone kept her thoughts to herself it was Sara.

For a moment Mrs. Wayne too said nothing. Then she roused herself from what were evidently unpleasant reflections and spoke again.

"If this really is final, of course there won't be any— any need for the elaborate trousseau we had planned. But, at the same time, I don't want to *seem* to accept this ridiculous decision of hers. Perhaps it would be best not to start anything new, Miss Farman. But I would certainly like you to complete whatever you have already begun."

"That will keep me busy for at least ten days," Beverley assured her.

"And by then perhaps Sara may have come to her senses," Mrs. Wayne said, but without much optimism in her voice. "Well, Miss Farman, we shall just have to wait and see what happens."

She turned away. But, as she reached the door, it opened suddenly and Sara herself came into the room.

"Oh—" she drew back slightly at the sight of her mother—"I—I didn't know you were here."

"I was just going." Mrs Wayne spoke a little coldly. "And if you came to tell Miss Farman that your trousseau will not be needed, I have already discussed this matter with her."

"Oh—no. It wasn't that." Sara looked only slightly abashed. "It was that I—I just heard her news from Toni, and I came to find out if it were true."

"Miss Farman's news?" It was obvious that in her preoccupation with her own unhappy problems, Mrs. Wayne had not taken in much of what her youngest child had so eagerly poured out. "Has Miss Farman some news?"

"Why, yes. I—believe so." Sara looked at Beverley with wide eyes.

"I think," Beverley heard herself say in a calm voice, "you must mean the reconciliation between

Geoffrey and his father. In an indirect way, I suppose it is my news too."

"Geoffrey? Geoffrey Revian?" Miss Wayne's tone expressed the minimum of interest. Indeed, a sort of annoyed surprise crept into her voice, as though in protest that anyone should put forward this item of news as noteworthy at a time when so much else of import was happening.

"Then it's true?" Sara said quickly.

"Yes. It's true. Geoffrey was sent for last night, as his father was very ill. There was a complete reconciliation, it seems, and today his father is a little better. He—sent for me, as he wanted to see—" she raised her eyes and looked across at Sara—"the girl Geoffrey was going to marry."

"And you—went?"

"Of course."

"And he—liked you?—He could hardly do anything else." Sara answered her own question, and in the same flatteringly simple terms as Toni. "This will make a—a great difference for you, Beverley, won't it?" The older Wayne girls tended to call Beverley by her Christian name, even though their mother remained on more formal terms.

"Not in the essentials," Beverley said quietly. "At least, I hope not."

"But Geoffrey's prospects—his whole position—will be altered. Instead of being an impecunious artist, struggling along on his own, he'll be the accepted only son of a wealthy father. You can't say that doesn't make a great difference in your life."

"I said it wouldn't make a difference in the essentials." Beverley smiled faintly. "I was never marrying Geoffrey for his social or financial prospects."

"Well—no." Sara pushed back her hair distractedly. "I realize that." She was silent for a moment, and at this point Mrs. Wayne, who evidently found the conversation not specially interesting, went away, leaving the two girls together.

Beverley proceeded to pack up the work she had allegedly come to fetch.

"So Mother has told you my news?" Sara stood watching her.

"Yes."

"What did you—think of it?"

"I don't quite know, Sara. I'm sorry to hear of any happy engagement going wrong. And I think that in many ways you and Franklin Lowell suited each other. But as I don't know your reason for breaking the engagement, I can't really venture an opinion."

"I never really—loved him, you know."

"Are you sure of that?"

"Quite sure."

There was a pause.

"Then I don't think there is anything else to say," Beverley told her at last. "For Franklin is much too worth-while a person to be fobbed off with less than the best."

"That's how I feel," said Sara, but rather perfunctorily, Beverley thought. Indeed, she doubted if Franklin's claim to consideration had found much place in Sara's reckoning.

"Your decision is quite final, I take it?" Beverley, who had packed up her work by now and was ready to go, looked across at the other girl levelly.

"Oh, yes! I'm absolutely determined about it. More so than ever now."

"Why do you say that?" asked Beverley sharply.

"Oh, I—don't know. I just meant that I—I'd had time to think things over during the day, to argue it out with the family."

"I see," said Beverley. "I'm afraid I must go now. I have to catch my bus."

She knew quite well that she had more than ample time to catch the next bus, but she felt suddenly that she could not stand there talking any longer to Sara, or she would have to start asking frantic, angry, impossible questions. Her self-control was wearing thin, and it was time to go, before she said anything which might precipitate another crisis.

Perhaps Sara vaguely felt this too. Or perhaps she

genuinely had forgotten about bus time. Anyway, she made no objection to Beverley's departure.

On the way downstairs she met no one, and in the hall there was only Toni, to bid her a friendly and slightly conspiratorial goodbye. But as she hurried unnecessarily down the lane, Beverley met the third of the Wayne sisters, slowly and aimlessly wandering up towards the house.

"Hello—" Madeleine greeted her dejectedly—"have you been up to the house?"

"Yes." Beverley once more went through the explanation about calling in to fetch some work she wanted to finish.

"It probably won't be needed now," Madeleine told her. "Have you heard the news?"

"About your sister's engagement? Yes."

"Isn't it the absolute limit?" Madeleine kicked a stone in a rather childish way. "What does she suppose is going to happen to the rest of us now? So much depended on this marriage of hers."

"Perhaps," Beverley could not help saying, "she felt that, in her own marriage, her own interests came first."

"Oh, yes—of course—in a way. But Franklin was ideal! As a husband, as a brother-in-law and as an addition to the family in every way. He was so generous, and easy-going. Who else do you suppose would have offered to pay for me at the Dramatic Academy, for one thing?"

"No one that I know of," Beverley said candidly. "But I don't imagine that he will withdraw that offer, once it has been made."

"*Don't* you?" Madeleine stopped kicking the stone and brightened up enormously at this suggestion. "I never thought of that. I supposed that he'd be so mad with the lot of us that he'd just wash his hands of us."

"But do you really think he is like that?" Beverley said, surprised that anyone could know Franklin Lowell so long and misread him so completely.

"I don't know," Madeleine confessed. "He's very proud, in his way, you know. And men do hate having their pride stepped on."

139

"Yes, of course. But—when you said he is generous, you were quite right. It's the outstanding thing about him. And I don't mean only material generosity. Lots of people manage to be that, and yet they are spiritually mean."

"Well—perhaps you're right." Madeleine considered that and became still more cheerful. "Oh, Beverley, if you see him, will you sound him, for me? I can't very well go to him myself, at this moment, whereas you——"

"I don't see that I can either," put in Beverley hastily.

"Oh, not specifically for that reason, of course. But you're bound to see him in the next few days. He calls in to see your mother sometimes, doesn't he?" And Madeleine looked at her curiously.

"Yes, sometimes. How did you know?"

"He mentioned it himself once. He says she's a wonderful woman."

"Well—she is, rather." Beverley smiled and flushed with pleasure. "What do you want me to say, if I do see him?"

"Oh, I leave it to you. You're clever at these things, I'm sure. Bring me into the conversation somehow, and say something about my—my hopes and ambitions ——" Madeleine bit her lip suddenly, perhaps at the thought of how those hopes and ambitions were being threatened. "Just find out for me—*please*, Beverley, find out for me—what he is going to do about his offer to me, now that I'm not going to be his sister-in-law."

"Well, I'll do my best," Beverley promised. "Though, mind—" she warned Madeleine—"I'm not prepared to say anything which will sound as though I think his chief rôle is that of general provider of good things."

"No, of course not," Madeleine agreed. "That would put him off more thoroughly than anything else," she added, a little naïvely.

Then she went on her way towards the house, obviously in much better spirits, while Beverley continued in the direction of her bus-stop.

As she reached this and stood there waiting, she could

not help recalling the first time she had waited there, and how Franklin Lowell had come along to offer her a lift. And, at that moment, almost as though her recollections forced history to repeat itself, a long, handsome open car came spinning round the corner, braked to a sudden stop, and Franklin Lowell called out to her,

"Hello! The bus won't be along for another twenty minutes. Jump in and I'll drive you home."

"Oh, thank you!" Beverley got into the seat beside him. "I was just thinking of you."

"How gratifying." He flashed her a quick smile, and then added—a trifle defiantly, she thought—"You've just come from the Grange, I take it?—and so you will have heard the news."

"Yes. I'm very sorry."

He shrugged and stared straight ahead, down the road in front of him.

"Is it a—very bad blow?" she asked diffidently, after a moment.

"No man likes being jilted," he replied dryly.

"No, of course not. I suppose what I meant was—did the whole thing come as a great shock, as something completely unexpected?"

He did not answer that immediately. Then he said slowly,

"I thought it did at first, Beverley. But, now that I've had time to think things over, I've looked back and seen that there were—signs of it coming. I have a feeling I've been a bit stupid about the whole business. And that's not a feeling that any man likes to have either."

"No. I can understand that. It's a blow to one's pride. But—" she gave him a searching glance—"was it a fearful blow to your—your affections too?"

"I was—I am—very fond of Sara," he said quickly. "It wasn't just a question of wanting a beautiful wife to grace my home, you know."

"Of course not. Though if that element was there, I think it was quite legitimate. But—forgive me if I'm jumping to conclusions—you don't sound absolutely heartbroken to me."

"Don't I?" He frowned. Then he gave her that flashing, rather dangerous smile. "But I'm not sure that hearts do break in real life, are you?"

"I don't know," said Beverley soberly, and she wondered if she would feel less than heartbroken if she had to lose Geoffrey. "But I take it, from your tone, that at least you have completely accepted Sara's decision?"

"Of course. What else could I do?"

"I suppose some men would have pleaded with her to reconsider things."

"I am not the pleading kind," he replied dryly. And since Beverley was sure this was all too true, there seemed nothing more to say about the broken engagement.

There was a short silence. Then he said something about Geoffrey's projected exhibition, and she roused herself to tell him of the new development.

Franklin listened with characteristically close attention, and then said thoughtfully,

"So Geoffrey has, overnight, been transformed from a struggling artist, with little backing, into an approved only son of an influential father? Quite a big change in his life."

"Yes."

"And in yours too."

"Perhaps." She could not imagine why it was that she always tended to show Franklin Lowell the real state of her thoughts, rather than the courageously determined façade which she presented to other people.

"Why do you say that?" he asked. "What happens to Geoffrey is bound to affect you too, isn't it?"

"I don't know." Inexplicably she was impelled to be frank with him. It even soothed her, in some strange way, to allow herself the indulgence of putting her anxiety into words.

"Do you remember," she said slowly, "that I told you once that I was afraid of someone else in his life?— that I believed he had been very fond of another girl?"

"Yes, of course. You saw him kiss her, that night

at the ball, and got the wind up enough to cry about it."

His tone was teasing, but it was not unkindly.

"So I did! I suppose that was silly of me." She smiled faintly and bit her lip. "But—it was a bit of a shock. Nowadays I think I can look at things more objectively——"

"Oh, my dear! One never does, with the people who really matter, you know," he protested.

"Sara, for instance?"

"Sara? We weren't talking about Sara."

"We were a little while back, and you have no idea how objective you contrived to sound."

"Did I?" He gave a rather vexed little laugh. "Well, go on with what you were saying about Geoffrey and his changed circumstances. You were going to tell me why they might not affect you."

"In one sense, they might affect me profoundly, I suppose," Beverley said deliberately. "But not in the way you mean. He might decide he didn't want to marry me after all."

"He couldn't be such a fool!"

"Oh——" Beverley laughed slightly at his vehemence —"I don't mean that he would think any less of me because his own position had improved. But—I don't know why I'm telling you this, except that I *have* to say it to someone other than myself!—I think it was poverty and his precarious position which put up the barrier between him and—and that other girl. The barrier is gone now——" She stopped speaking, but she completed her sentence with a gesture of her hands which seemed to indicate the infinity of possibilities now presented.

"You forget one thing. He has chosen you to share his life. He didn't have to choose anyone. If he was so crazy about this other girl, I suppose he could have just remained faithful to her memory."

"Lots of men make themselves contented with a second-best," she replied doggedly, though it hurt badly to put that thought into words.

"True, but——" he glanced at her dryly—"you never struck me as any man's second-best."

"Oh——" she laughed a little—"thank you."

"And there's one other thing you have forgotten. I'd forgotten it too until this moment. You told me that other girl was married."

"Married?" For a moment Beverley looked completely blank, for she had entirely forgotten how she had invented this detail, in order to forestall any suspicions Franklin might have had of the real identity of the other girl in Geoffrey's life. "Married? Oh, no. She——" Suddenly Beverley stopped and put her hand to her mouth in dismay. "Oh——" she said, and then all powers of inspiration or invention seemed to dry up

"So she wasn't married?" said Franklin thoughtfully.

"N-no."

"Odd that you should have been so sure of that, when you last told me about her. Or did you just invent that?"

"I invented it. I didn't want you to start guessing. It —it wouldn't have been fair to anyone," Beverley explained hastily.

"But was I at all likely to guess? Do I know her?"

"I—I'd rather not say."

But he went on, thinking aloud.

"At the time of the ball, it was so vitally necessary I should not know that you even invented this story. You were willing that I should regard Geoffrey as philandering with a married woman rather than that I should identify the girl. And yet now it matters so little that you even forgot you had ever told me that tale."

"Please don't bother to—to work it out like that. It doesn't matter. It's not all that important. It——"

"Wait a minute." He drew the car to a standstill at the side of the road and turned to regard her in a way that agitated her. "I think it *is* important."

"No, really! Please don't think any more about it. I shouldn't even have told you so much. I don't know why I did. It's—it's disloyal, in a way, and——"

"Of course!" he explained suddenly, as though she had not uttered a word of protest. "What a fool I've been not to guess it before. The girl was Sara, wasn't it?"

CHAPTER TEN

"IT was Sara who was the girl in the background of Geoffrey's life, wasn't it?" Franklin repeated, as Beverley remained obstinately silent. "That was why you were so afraid I might guess something, while she was still engaged to me."

"Yes," Beverley said slowly at last. "I suppose there's no harm in telling you now. But at the time of the ball I just couldn't let you know. It was bad enough to indulge in anxieties and suspicions myself, but I had no right to communicate them to anyone else. Least of all, to someone so personally concerned. Besides, I didn't even know if the suspicions were well founded. I don't even know now, come to that," she added, with a sigh.

"But what you really think is that Geoffrey was the man Sara loved, only she wouldn't marry him so long as he was a poor man?"

"It sounds so—brutal, put like that, but——"

"The truth often sounds brutal," Franklin assured her dryly.

"I think—in fact, I know—that Sara was—was greatly attracted to Geoffrey. And I can't imagine that he didn't feel *something* very deep for her. Otherwise, why should he kiss her even after he had become engaged to me? But I don't think marriage was ever even discussed between them. It was not a practical possibility."

"And—now?" He bit his lip thoughtfully.

"Now it has become so," said Beverley simply. "That's all there is to it. I should be unrealistic if I didn't face the fact."

He stared at her moodily for a moment, then those bold, fine eyes of his softened, and he said,

"You're a brave girl. Do you think this was why Sara threw me over?"

"No. I'm sure it wasn't. She didn't know about Geoffrey's changed circumstances until I told her—or,

145

rather, Toni told her—an hour ago. It was just one of those coincidences that happen only in real life."

"I'm glad of that," he said slowly. "I'd have hated to think she just snatched shamelessly at the best of both worlds. I'll be glad to remember that she drew back from marrying me simply because she couldn't face the substitute thing, after all."

"It couldn't have been easy," Beverley agreed. "I think the family are all pretty mad with her. Except Toni, of course." And she smiled.

"Toni doesn't grind her own axe," agreed Franklin, with a slight smile in his turn, allowing by implication that the others did. "Maybe she's too young to have learned how."

"Oh, no. She is naturally and truly interested in what happens to other people. She always will be," Beverley asserted. "But that doesn't mean that I'm criticizing the rest of them. In fact, if it wouldn't sound impertinent at such a time, I'd say—don't think too hardly of Sara."

"I don't." He turned his head and smiled full at Beverley. "And if I felt tempted to do so, I'd remind myself that you don't appear to be thinking too harshly of Geoffrey, which must be more difficult still.—What are you going to do about this new turn of events, Beverley?"

"I don't know."

"Just let things take their course?"

"Oh, not—that. I think I'll have to—to put the issue to the test, in some way."

"It will take some courage."

"It would take more to face the prospect of just going on, for ever wondering what the real truth was," Beverley retorted.

"Well, perhaps you're right." But he frowned. "I wish I could help you somehow."

"Why, how nice of you!" She smiled at him, a good deal touched. "I guess it's something I just have to tackle myself, but it gives one a good feeling to know that someone sympathetic is in the background."

"Anyway—" he started the car again—"use me if you need me. I'm feeling a bit out on a limb, at the moment, and I suppose it would soothe my pride a bit to know that I was essential to someone's planning. Selfish, of course, but you may as well profit by it, if it's of any use to you."

"I will." Beverley laughed softly and accepted his casual explanation of his offer at its face value. But at heart she was touched afresh by what she guessed to be his genuine sympathy.

He drove her home after that, but refused her invitation to come in.

"Your mother and you will have enough to talk about, without a third person there," he declared. And she saw no reason to tell him that she had chosen to keep her mother in happy ignorance of the complications in her life.

Indeed, as soon as she re-entered the house, Beverley found it necessary to resume the rôle of the happy fiancée whose future was looking exceptionally rosy.

"How did you get on with him?" Aunt Ellen wanted to know immediately, not even specifying who the all-important "him" might be. And she followed Beverley into her mother's room, determined not to miss a word of the story.

"How is Mr. Revian, darling?" Beverley's mother looked at her anxiously. "You look a bit pale and strained."

"Oh, I'm all right." Beverley put up her hands and rubbed some colour into her cheeks, and Aunt Ellen said, "I'll get you a cup of tea in a minute. But—what happened?"

"Nothing very much. Except that I was taken to see Mr. Revian, and he spoke kindly to me, and seemed quite—pleased with Geoffrey's choice."

"I wouldn't call that 'nothing very much,' " declared Aunt Ellen. "I'd call that very satisfactory. You mean that he knows all about the engagement and he approves?"

"I think so—yes. He referred to Grandfather very flatteringly. Said he was the best man he ever heard in the pulpit, and a grand worker in the parish too."

"That's true," agreed Aunt Ellen with emphasis.

"Though he was a little on the easy-going side with some who needed a firm hand. Still, Mr. Revian wouldn't know that. Go on, Beverley—what else happened?"

"I stayed to lunch, and met Geoffrey's aunt——"

"How did *she* react?" Aunt Ellen displayed an almost professional interest in aunts.

"Politely rather than cordially, but that may just be her manner."

"No, no. She's jealous, mark my words. She'll make trouble if she can." Aunt Ellen wagged her head in gloomy satisfaction.

"Oh, Ellen, don't be tiresome! Why should she?" exclaimed Mrs. Farman impatiently.

"Because she feels her own nose will be put out of joint, of course. But, in a way, that's a good sign. She wouldn't bother to be resentful if she thought Beverley would soon be pushed out of the way."

"I wouldn't describe her as resentful," said Beverley mildly. "Merely unenthusiastic."

"Well, they seem to have kept you there long enough, anyway, dear." Beverley's mother smiled encouragingly at her daughter. "You must have stayed a good while after lunch."

"Oh, no, I didn't, really. I met Toni Wayne on the bus and—I called in at the Grange with her."

"Why?" asked Aunt Ellen, who always liked to get straight to the bottom of things. "To tell them about Geoffrey's father?"

"Not exactly," said Beverley disingenuously. "I went to collect some work I'd like to finish this evening. Besides—Toni had told me some rather distressing news. Sara has broken off her engagement."

"Broken off her engagement? Then they won't want you working for them any more," cried Aunt Ellen, unerringly selecting the blackest outlook from a personal point of view.

"I don't know about that. For the moment, I am to go on with what I have already begun. But—no, I suppose they won't want me for as long as I expected."

"That's the least of it," declared Mrs. Farman, "especially as you're getting married so soon yourself.

But I'm dreadfully sorry. Did you hear what the trouble was? How could she *not* want to marry that nice Franklin Lowell, I wonder?"

"I think she just decided she didn't love him, after all," Beverley said cautiously.

"With all that money—and a fine estate?" Aunt Ellen laughed sceptically. "She's probably found someone who is a better catch. Though how—and who it could be—" she frowned as she obviously passed the cream of the county in hurried mental review—"I really don't know. I'll go and see about some tea now."

And, satisfied that she had heard all the salient points of Beverley's news, she hurried off into the kitchen.

"Will he take it very badly, Beverley?" Mrs. Farman, who had developed quite a genuine affection for Franklin Lowell, looked solemn.

"He is feeling pretty miserable at the moment, I think. He brought me home just now, and we talked about the broken engagement quite frankly," Beverley explained. "But, at a guess, I'd say his pride has suffered more than his heart."

"Pride can hurt an awful lot too," remarked Mrs. Farman, but she smiled slightly. "*Was* there someone else, Beverley?"

"Someone else?"

"I mean—did Sara Wayne decide that she wanted another man whatever the reason?"

Beverley hesitated a moment. Then she said curiously.

"I wonder what makes you ask that?"

"It's always a reason for a broken engagement—or one of the reasons. But, in this case, it seems the most likely reason to me. Franklin Lowell is a rather special person, quite apart from his worldly advantages. It would be quite extraordinarily difficult *not* to fall in love with him, I'd say, unless there were a strong counter-attraction. And as for falling out of love with him——No, no, Sara Wayne must have had a very definite feeling for someone other than Franklin."

"Oh, Mother, do you think so?" Beverley tried not to feel dejected and failed.

"So it seems to me. But there's no need to look

glum about it, darling. Once one has accepted the fact that she has broken the engagement, I suppose the reason why is immaterial."

"I suppose so," Beverley managed to say. But she was glad that Aunt Ellen chose this moment to come in again with the tea.

During the evening Aunt Ellen became almost cheerful. Local affairs were of infinitely more interest to her than world affairs, and she had a wonderful time examining Sara Wayne's broken engagement from every point of view. But it was only when she remarked, "This will make a great deal of difference to the other Wayne girls too," that Beverley remembered guiltily that she had forgotten to ask Franklin what he intended to do about Madeleine's year at the Dramatic Academy.

"There will be another chance," she assured herself remorsefully. "And there *are* rather a lot of other things to think about at the moment."

Once or twice that evening she was severely tempted to go out to the telephone box and ring up Geoffrey, just to hear his voice and gain some reassurance from the sound of it. But if she did that, she would feel bound to tell him of Sara's broken engagement. And what she wanted above all else was to be able to *see* him when he first received that news.

It was possible, of course, that Sara would herself telephone and tell him, but, on the whole, Beverley thought that unlikely. And so she waited, through an uneventful evening and a rather restless night, alternately hoping for the best and trying to face the possibility of the worst happening.

Early the next morning, the respectful chauffeur in the big car came to fetch her once more to Castleton. Mr. Revian was a little better again, it seemed, but he would like to see Beverley once more. Mr. Geoffrey had not been able to come himself because he was reluctant to leave his father. If Miss Farman wouldn't mind——

Miss Farman said she did not mind at all. And, having bade her mother and aunt a hasty goodbye, she stepped into the big car and was driven away in state, while one or two stragglers from early morning service stood in the main street of Binwick and gazed after her in pleasant speculation.

The car was very beautiful and very comfortable, and Beverley leaned back in her seat, trying hard to relax. But she knew, from the way her hands kept on clasping each other tightly, that she was feeling nervous again. Not because of the prospect of seeing old Mr. Revian this time. But because she knew that she was nearing the vital test of her relationship with Geoffrey.

It was he himself who came out to greet her, and his welcoming hug and kiss should have been reassuring enough. But when he led her into the library and said, "The old man's asleep at the moment," she knew that here was the opportunity which she had to grasp.

For a minute or two they talked of Geoffrey's father and the slight improvement which had taken place since Beverley had been there the previous day. Then, at a momentary pause in the conversation, she heard herself say quite calmly,

"I met Toni when I was going back on the bus yesterday."

"Toni Wayne? Did you? That gave you lively company, I'll bet. She always has plenty to say for herself."

"Yes. She had even more than usual to tell me yesterday." Beverley paused for a second, with the queer sensation that she was about to launch herself into space from a great height. Then, though she looked straight at Geoffrey, she spoke almost casually. "It seems that Sara has broken off her engagement"

"Sara!—broken—her engagement?"

She was not really surprised that Geoffrey had lost colour. Only a sort of leaden despair seemed to replace the anguish of uncertainty.

"You mean—she's not going to marry Lowell, after all?"

"Yes, that's what I mean. She is not going to marry Franklin Lowell," said Beverley quite exactly.

"But—" suddenly he got up and walked from one side of the room to the other—"why not?" His voice

151

had gone hoarse. "What reason does she give? I mean—
what reason did Toni give?"

"None. Except that she just doesn't want to marry
him, after all. That was the reason Sara herself gave,
when I saw her later."

"Then you—you've seen her?"

"Oh, yes. I called in at the Grange on my way home."

"And—talked to her about this broken engagement?"

"A little. She was not inclined to say very much,
naturally. We aren't intimate friends after all."

"So that—you say—you have no idea why she did
this?"

"No, I didn't say that. I said Sara herself gave no
specific reason. But," Beverley went on, not knowing
whether a sense of justice, or sheer nervousness, or just
stupidity prompted the next words, "my own view has
always been that Sara really wanted someone else. Not
Franklin Lowell at all."

"I—wonder what made you think that." Geoffrey
had sat down again now, opposite her, but she had the
queer impression that his defences were down. His
clasped hands hung slackly between his knees and his
face looked pale and drawn.

"Quite a number of small incidents combined to make
me think it, I suppose," she said slowly. "At one time
I thought it was best to—ignore the fact, to put a line
under the past. But now—it's different, isn't it?"

He didn't reply. He just stared at her, half appre-
hensively, so that she was suddenly bitterly sorry for
him. Much more sorry than for herself. And it was
not at all difficult to say quite gently.

"It was you she wanted, wasn't it, Geoffrey? And if
things had been as they are now, it's you who would
have been engaged to her."

"Oh, Beverley—" he gave a little groan and buried
his face in his hands—"how did you guess?"

"I told you—there were lots of things—but none
of them matters now. The only thing which matters
is the fact that you and Sara love each other, and
the barriers are down."

"But I can't do this to you! You've been such a dear,

loyal, loving girl, all the years I've known you." He looked up haggardly. "That's why I thought——"

"You thought you could make a good second-best of things with me, didn't you?" She spoke without bitterness. "You probably would have too—if Sara had been permanently out of the running. But that isn't how things are, Geoffrey."

"They—could be still," he said, but without conviction.

"Oh, no, dear!" She got up and came and stood beside him. "You don't think we could really go on from here, do you? Not even if I would accept such a sacrifice—which of course I wouldn't. You couldn't marry me now, just out of friendship and a sort of mistaken sense of chivalry. Any more than I could marry you, now that I know it's Sara you really want."

"But—what are we to do?"

"Just break our engagement and—and call it a day. Then you can go to Sara and—and tell her you're free. It's almost simple, really."

"No, it isn't. There's the old man to consider." Dismayed recollection flooded into Geoffrey's face. "He's taken an enormous fancy to you. He talked of little else when I was with him yesterday evening and this morning. He says you're the ideal girl for me, and that you've been the making of me—and other rather chastening things."

Geoffrey grinned faintly for a moment, but then he became serious again.

"I can't imagine what sort of a shock it would be for him, Beverley, to find I really wanted—I mean—that I proposed to marry someone else, after all. It would be enough to give him another heart attack. Quite apart from the fact that he'd decide I was an irresponsible rotter, after all. Which I suppose I am," he added ruefully.

"Nonsense. Circumstances have just been unfortunate. But—do you really think he would take it so hard?"

"I think it could even threaten the new harmony between us."

"Then what are we to do?" She looked blank in her turn.

"I don't know. That's what I was asking you just now," Geoffrey said gloomily. And at this moment the nurse came into the room to announce that Mr. Revian was awake and would be very happy to see Miss Farman.

"All right. I'm coming——" Beverley made a movement towards the door. But Geoffrey exclaimed.

"Wait a moment! We've got to settle this first."

"Can't we discuss it afterwards?"

"No. We've got to know what we are going to do— from now on. He must wait a few minutes. Ask my father to wait a few minutes, Nurse. Miss Farman won't be long."

"Very well, Mr. Revian." The nurse gazed severely into space. "But I wouldn't delay too much, you know. He doesn't stay very bright for long at a time."

"I won't be long," Beverley promised, and the nurse went out of the room again.

Geoffrey was pacing about once more, in nervous agitation. And, looking at him, Beverley had the distinct impression that it would be she who would have to take the initiative.

"It isn't really that he's weak," she told herself quickly and defensively. "It's just that everything has happened so suddenly. And everything that matters to him is trembling in the balance."

Aloud she said, "Will you trust me to handle the situation in my own way?"

"You mean—tell him the whole thing now?"

"Not exactly as it is—no. And not unless I see a good opening and feel that I can lessen the shock. But let me see him alone——"

"I think that's what he wants, in any case."

"And leave me to do the best I can."

"Remember that he must not have a severe shock. And—the reconciliation is very real, Beverley, but it's a new and rather fragile plant."

"I'll remember."

"Bless you!" He caught her hand suddenly and held

it against his cheek. "You're the dearest and most wonderful friend. I feel sick with myself for hurting you so much."

She pulled her hand away quickly. She had to do that, or she would have begun to cry. And then, because her pride had received all the battering it could stand, she said coolly,

"Don't think of me as too desperately hurt, Geoffrey. If it's any consolation to you, I had already begun to wonder if—" she stopped, groped for something that would not be too hurtful—"if I had really allowed myself to become engaged to the right man."

He stared at her.

"Do you mean," he said almost hopefully, "that there was someone else with you, too?"

"Oh, I—don't want to be too explicit at this moment. But—" somehow she managed quite a provocative little smile—"don't feel too badly about it all."

And then she went out of the room and upstairs to old Mr. Revian, aware that she had left a half-puzzled, half-relieved Geoffrey behind her.

She had little time to arrange any plan of campaign. She must just trust to her own ingenuity and good sense. And she must accept the fact that, unless a good opportunity presented itself, she would do best to possess her soul in patience and delay any form of explanation for a few days longer, rather than risk saying too much too soon.

The nurse was in the room when Beverley entered, but she rose and took her departure almost immediately—probably on previous instructions, Beverley thought.

"Come here, my dear. Come and sit down by the bed." The old man's voice sounded stronger that morning. "I want to have a talk with you."

Beverley came and sat down in the chair indicated, and smiled upon Mr. Revian with all the tranquil good humour she could achieve.

"You're better. I can see that," she said. And he nodded briefly, but dismissed this as of no special importance.

"I want to talk to you about Geoffrey." He plunged into the subject without preamble. "You understand him and manage him very well, I notice——"

"I've known him a great many years," Beverley interrupted with a smile. "Ever since I was a little girl. We're very good friends, Geoffrey and I. We always shall be."

"Well—that's quite a good basis for a marriage, I suppose." Geoffrey's father smiled. "And I hope the boy's as stable in his attitude towards you. I suppose you know——" he shot a shrewd look at her—"that he's not the strongest of characters?"

"He is essentially good and decent," Beverley said quietly.

"Hm, yes. I think he's that. But if you marry him ——"

"Mr. Revian, have you any doubt about that?" Beverley smiled at him.

"No, no. Just a manner of speaking. You mustn't take offence so easily!"

"I wasn't taking offence," said Beverley slowly. "In an odd way, I was relieved."

"Relieved?" The old man looked astonished. "Why?"

"Because Geoffrey thinks you regard this marriage as signed and sealed and the only thing possible for the happiness of all of us. Although three days ago you didn't even know of my existence, Geoffrey seems to think it would be an almost mortal blow to you if you couldn't have me for a daughter-in-law. No one's well-being should be *so* much dependent on another person, should it?"

"Well—no—of course not." He looked disturbed and rather healthily annoyed, Beverley thought. "Mortal blow, indeed! No, no, I wouldn't use a term like that. But this is quite an academic argument, I take it——"

"No, Mr. Revian. It isn't—entirely. And that's why I'm glad of the chance to talk to you. Whatever my faults may be—and I have a number—at least I'm straight with the people I like. And I like you."

There was a moment's silence. Then he said gruffly, "I like you too, come to that. So you can be as

156

straight as you like with me. What is it you want to say? Something I won't want to hear? That's usually what people mean when they say they're going to do some straight talking."

She smiled slightly, but she put up a silent little prayer that she might find the right words.

"Mr. Revian, have you ever been quite, quite sure of something in your life, and then found out, after all, that you were wrong?"

Again he shot her that penetrating glance.

"I suppose so—yes. Most people have, if they're honest with themselves."

"Well, that really happened with Geoffrey and me. We'd known and liked each other so long that we both thought—honestly—that we would be happy married to each other. That's why we got engaged, some months ago now. But then, quite recently, we both had the same experience. We met someone else——"

"*Both* of you?" The old man looked sceptical.

"Both of us," Beverley insisted firmly. "Neither knew about the other, and right up to yesterday, we both meant to stand by our bargain. You see, we were truly too fond of each other—as friends—to be able to face letting each other down. But then, yesterday——"

"Yes? What happened yesterday?" asked Mr. Revian, as she paused.

"I suppose," Beverley said slowly, "that when one is under an emotional strain—and Geoffrey particularly was, after the happiness of being reconciled to you— one is not so good at hiding one's feelings. Somehow we came to talk frankly to each other, Geoffrey and I— and we found that, while we shall always be fond of each other as friends, we both want to marry someone else."

"You both——" The old man swallowed, and for a moment Beverley wondered if she had gone too far and too fast.

"Please, please don't mind too much," she begged him. "Or else I shall feel a wicked, selfish girl, instead of a very happy one."

Again there was silence, while Beverley held her breath. Then he said, rather disagreeably,

"So you'll always be good friends, eh, in the modern way?"

"Oh, yes, of course! And it's not specially modern. We've *been* friends for years. There's no reason why we shouldn't go on being so."

"Does that mean that you'll go on being friends with me?" he demanded with a grim smile.

"Yes, please." Beverley leaned forward and kissed his cheek lightly, which seemed to surprise and please him immensely.

"I've a suspicion you're a minx," he said. "Well, who *is* the girl that my boy is going to marry?"

"A perfectly lovely girl called Sara Wayne."

"Of Huntingford Grange?"

"Yes."

"Father's a bit of a mountebank, but her mother's good stock," was the slightly disagreeable comment on this. "And who are you going to marry?"

"I?"

"Yes, you. You've got a part in this double romance too, haven't you? Unless you've been foxing me with some story all the time." And he gave her such an unexpectedly penetrating look that Beverley felt herself tremble.

"Of course I haven't been 'foxing' you, as you call it. Why should I?" she protested.

"In order to shield that boy of mine," was the devastatingly shrewd retort. "You can't tell me much about him, you know, even though I'm confoundedly glad to be friends with him again. But I'll not have him behave badly to a girl of your calibre. Not if I have to turn him out of the house again."

"But you mustn't even think of doing that!" cried Beverley in great alarm, "You'd spoil everything for—for all of us."

"And who are 'all of us?'" was the dry enquiry.

"Why, Geoffrey and Sara, and me and—and——"

"Yes? Who?"

She thought for a wild moment of saying, "John

Smith," but she knew that no fictitious creature was going to satisfy this rather terrifying and angry old man. She had to find somebody genuine—somebody who would do as a sort of "stand-in" in this emergency. Somebody—but who?

And then—quite distinctly and with complete reassurance she recalled Franklin Lowell saying, only yesterday, "Use me if you need me. I suppose it would soothe my pride a bit to know I was essential to someone's plans."

He had not meant it so literally, of course. But she could not even wait to think what an outrageous thing she was doing. She took a deep breath and said very calmly,

"I didn't really want to tell anyone yet. Not until we had actually fixed things up. But—I'm going to marry Franklin Lowell."

CHAPTER ELEVEN

"FRANKLIN LOWELL?" repeated old Mr. Revian in an astonished tone. "Do you mean Franklin Lowell of Elthorpe Hall?"

"Yes," said Beverley resolutely, though her heart really quaked when she thought what she was committing herself to.

"That's a very fine match for you, isn't it?" The old man spoke bluntly.

"I suppose it is," she agreed, wondering now why on earth she could not have instanced someone much less distinguished and much harder to identify.

"And you're telling me that you and he are more or less engaged?"

"Like Geoffrey and Sara—yes." She saw no point in watering down her statement now. She had made it, and she had better stick to it. It was not as though Mr. Revian, ill in bed, could make any real investigation or provoke any crisis. To him the situation was of interest only in so far as it affected Geoffrey's story.

At least, that was how Beverley profoundly hoped it would be.

For a moment or two there was silence. Then he said slowly,

"Well, if you tell me that's how things are, there isn't much I can do about it, I suppose, but accept the position. But I'm sorry you're not going to marry my boy. I think you'd have been the making of him."

"The girl he really wants will be the making of him," Beverley managed to assure Geoffrey's father with a smile. "That's how it is with any man."

"Depends what sort of girl he wants," retorted old Mr. Revian dryly.

"Well, Sara Wayne is the girl Geoffrey loves, and she is quite capable of bringing out the best in him," Beverley asserted, and in that moment she was fairly certain this was a fact.

"I hope you're right." Geoffrey's father was not

willing to be convinced in the first few minutes. "And now I suppose you want to go? You won't bother to come and see me, now that I'm no longer going to be your father-in-law."

"That doesn't follow at all. Geoffrey and I are remaining——"

"Yes, I know all about that. You've used that silly expression about remaining good friends once already," he admonished her impatiently. "And it doesn't really mean a thing. Or it shouldn't do so. If Geoffrey is going to marry Sara Wayne, he won't have much time or notice for the other girl he nearly married. And well you know it, since you're a sensible girl."

Beverley looked him straight in the eyes. Then she smiled, although she knew that she was saying her final goodbye to Geoffrey, in all that mattered, and she managed to say quite firmly,

"You're right, of course. It wouldn't be tactful for me to turn up here often in the near future. But that still doesn't mean you and I won't see anything of each other later. It just means that you will have to get well quickly, so that we can meet elsewhere."

"Are you trying to arrange some clandestine meeting with me?" he enquired, with a good deal of enjoyment.

"Not exactly." Beverley smiled. "But I promise you we will not lose sight of each other, even though I'm not going to be your—your daughter-in-law."

"All right. Though I suppose Franklin Lowell will be having the last word now on how your time is spent."

"Fra—— Oh, yes. Yes, of course. But I shall have some say in it too."

"I'll be bound you will!" He looked at her with approval still tinged with regret. "You're really what I mean by a girl of spirit. I'm sorry Geoffrey hadn't the sense to appreciate you. Yes—I'm truly sorry. And I only hope this Wayne girl is worth half as much as you."

"You'll love her," Beverley predicted confidently.

"How do you know? You don't know what I love," he retorted crossly. But he bade her a friendly goodbye after that. And Beverley went downstairs, with the curious feeling of having passed a stiff examination, without deriving much sense of elation from the fact.

Geoffrey was waiting for her at the foot of the stairs, and she had the impression that he must have been walking up and down the hall for some time—even possibly coming halfway up the stairs from time to time, in doubt whether or no he should interrupt the conversation.

"Well?" he said, too anxious to put his query less than crudely. "What happened?"

"Come into the library—or somewhere where we can talk more privately," she told him. And it was she who led the way into the silent, empty room where, half an hour ago, they had had their revealing discussion.

But she had no wish to keep him in suspense, and as soon as he had closed the door, she faced him and said,

"It's all right. I've told him everything."

"Everything?" Geoffrey looked slightly alarmed.

"Well—everything that was necessary." She pushed back her hair with an unconsciously weary little gesture. "I explained that we had mutually come to the conclusion that we really only—liked each other as very good friends, and that, in fact, we both wanted to marry someone else."

"Both?" Geoffrey said.

"I had to make it both. Otherwise he would have gone off the deep end, with some idea that you didn't value me at my real worth, and that you needed to be taught a lesson by him."

"Good lord!" Geoffrey looked rather disgusted.

"It was all rather melodramatic and Victorian at that point," Beverley conceded. "But I managed to imply that—that this was the way *I* wanted things too. I think he was genuinely disappointed that I was not going to belong to his family, after all. But I told him how lovely and charming Sara is——"

"You—you spoke about Sara personally?"

"Certainly. The sooner he knows about her, the better. Besides, it all sounded more real and convincing if I gave actual names. And maybe it left less for you to explain." She smiled at him, and it was the smile she might have used to someone much younger than herself.

"Oh, Beverley, how good you are——" He came near to her and took her hand, though really she would have much preferred him not to touch her. "I don't know what to say to you—how to thank you——"

"There's nothing to thank me for. I kept on telling him that you and I remained good friends, and it's true, I hope."

"Of course!"

"Well, I only did what a good friend should."

"And you don't think the shock was too much for him?"

"No. I think he was healthily annoyed at one or two points. But I saw no signs of physical strain because of it. In fact, he struck me as being a great deal brighter and more energetic than he was yesterday."

Geoffrey was silent for a moment, and she saw, from his expression, that he was slowly digesting the wonderful fact that he was free to take his happiness where he knew he would find it.

But, even then, he needed absolute reassurance. He said,

"You told him categorically that—that——"

"You and I are no longer engaged." She finished the sentence for him quite calmly. And, as though to give point to the words, she drew off the beautiful ring she had worn with so much pleasure and held it out to him.

"Oh, Beverley—I wish you'd keep the ring. It—it suits you somehow, and——"

"No dear. I couldn't do that, you know." She still spoke calmly, though she felt a great desire to break down and weep at this moment. "Please take it." And she put it on the desk beside him, since he seemed unable to go through the actual motions of taking back his ring.

"I also told your father that you and Sara will be announcing your engagement quite soon. And I hinted very strongly that I should be doing the same."

"With whom?" he asked quickly, and for a moment he looked startled and, in some quite illogical way, annoyed.

She hesitated for a fraction of a second. Then she said resolutely,

"He will probably mention it, if I don't tell you. I simply had to name someone, Geoffrey, or else your father wouldn't have accepted my story about this being a mutual arrangement. I—I told him I was going to marry Franklin Lowell."

"*Lowell?*—But you're—not, are you?"

"No, of course not. Don't be silly! I had to invent someone, I tell you. To—to name an actual person."

"Yes, I understand that. But—Lowell! It seems a bit near home, somehow. What's he going to say, if he ever hears of this?"

"He won't hear of it," said Beverley hastily. "You must see to that! Your father won't be in any position to talk to anyone in the outside world for some time. His life is bounded by his bedroom. He hasn't even a telephone there. And, long before this situation changes, he will have got used to your being engaged to Sara. Then presently, just as a matter of interest, you can let him know that—that my engagement didn't come to anything."

"He'll be upset about that."

"Well, then, he must *be* upset!" cried Beverley, who felt suddenly that she had done absolutely all she was capable of doing for the Revian family and that now they must look after themselves. "It won't be a matter of great moment to him by then. He hardly knows me, really, except as a girl he was very willing to accept into his family. He may be sorry for me—" she winced, because she was rather tired of being an object of pity and a cause for guilty feelings—"but it won't go further than that. He'll be enjoying his return to health by then, and I—I'll be making quite a new life of my own."

"Will you, Beverley?" He tried to take her hand again, but she avoided him. "Will you really not feel too badly about this? I'd like to think———"

"I'll manage splendidly," she told him coolly. "I'd

be a hypocrite if I pretended I was not quite badly hit by this. But that doesn't mean I shan't get over it one day and—and perhaps be very happy with someone else."

"Oh, my dear, I do hope so!"

Geoffrey said this from his heart, prompted no doubt as much by an obscure sense of guilt as by genuine good feeling.

They said goodbye after that. In a perfectly friendly spirit, but rather awkwardly, as though they had suddenly become well-disposed strangers, who had so little in common that it was difficult to know how to treat each other. Then Beverley went away to catch her bus. For in his agitation—or possibly his relief—Geoffrey forgot this time to suggest that she should be driven home in the car.

Beverley would have refused, even if the offer had been made. But somehow this tiny indication that his thoughts were already so little employed on her welfare made her feel indescribably dejected. Once more she sat in the front seat of the bus on the way home, and once or twice she had to put up her hand to wipe away an uncontrollable tear, for all the vanished hopes and dreams and joys that had been hers.

She reached home just in time for lunch, which surprised Aunt Ellen, who immediately suspected disaster, even before she noticed her niece's ringless left hand. However, at first she was too busy "dishing up" to make many enquiries, and it was not until they were all having coffee in Mrs. Farman's room after lunch that Aunt Ellen suddenly exclaimed,

"Beverley! You've lost your ring!"

"No, I haven't." Beverley spoke curtly, for she secretly dreaded another scene of explanation. "I've given it back."

"Given it back!" For once her mother and aunt spoke in unison, and her mother's tone was almost as dismayed as Aunt Ellen's.

"Do you mean that you—you have broken your engagement, dear?" her mother asked anxiously. While Aunt Ellen asserted with gloomy triumph.

"No, *he* has! Just as I said he would. Beverley isn't good enough for him now that he's a rich man."

"Oh, do be quiet, Ellen!" Mrs. Farman hardly ever spoke so sharply to her sister, even when goaded, and Aunt Ellen immediately assumed an expression of deep offence. "Let Beverley speak for herself. That is—if you want to tell us about it, darling," Mrs. Farman added.

"I shall have to tell you some time. It may as well be now." Beverley managed to make her voice sound very well controlled and matter-of-fact. "Geoffrey did not break the engagement. I did. And I did it because I found that he was really in love with someone else."

"Oh, my dear—" her mother put out a sympathetic hand to her—"I'm so sorry."

But Aunt Ellen, who simply could not maintain her offended silence in face of so many questions which were crying out to be asked, wagged her head critically and enquired,

"Why did he get engaged to you, then, if he really wanted someone else?"

"It was all a mistake, Aunt Ellen. People do make mistakes sometimes, you know, even about the things that matter most. You may as well know now. The other girl is Sara Wayne."

"Sara Wayne?" Is that why she broke off her engagement to Franklin Lowell? Nobody seems to know their own mind any more. I don't know what young folk are coming to," Aunt Ellen declared.

"They always made silly mistakes like this," her sister reminded her, but she looked grave. "Was this really why Sara broke her engagement, dear?"

"No." Beverley shook her head. "In a way, it was the other way round. When Geoffrey heard that she was free, he—he rather gave himself away. I had been suspecting something for—for a little while, and I asked him to be frank. You mustn't think he wasn't upset at—at having to hurt me. But once I knew what the true position was, of course there was only one thing to do."

"Of course," agreed her mother, but she sighed.

"And what has old Mr. Revian to say to all this?" enquired Aunt Ellen after a moment of blackest thought. "I suppose he's only too glad that Geoffrey is going to marry someone from the county instead of a village dressmaker?"

"On the contrary," said Beverley dryly, "he was a good deal annoyed and upset. I had to go to a great deal of elaborate explanation and some pretence to soften down the news sufficiently for him to accept it, in his weak state."

"Well, that's something," Aunt Ellen conceded grudgingly, the hurt to her family pride somewhat assuaged by the thought of Mr. Revian regretting the attractive Sara Wayne as a substitute for her niece.

There was silence for a moment. Then Mrs. Farman, who missed very little, asked somewhat diffidently,

"What did you mean by saying, dear, that you had to resort to a certain amount of pretence, when you explained things to old Mr. Revian?"

Beverley paused, chose her words carefully, and replied as casually as possible,

"He seemed ready to blame Geoffrey——"

"Quite right too," interjected Aunt Ellen.

"——And I had to imply that the arrangement was mutual. That, in fact, I was as anxious to break the engagement as he was."

"And how did you do that?" enquired her mother, with some curiosity.

"By telling him that I too had changed my mind and——and wanted to marry someone else."

"Who?" asked Aunt Ellen, on to that interesting point like a bird on a nice fat worm.

But fortunately, before Beverley could be driven to further dissembling, her mother answered for her.

"She doesn't mean that she mentioned anyone specifically, Ellen. Don't be silly! I suppose you just made a general statement, dear?"

Beverley smiled wanly and nodded vaguely, glad that her mother had never met Mr. Revian and therefore did not know how unlikely he was to be satisfied by any general statement.

After that there seemed little more to say on the melancholy subject, and Beverley was able to escape to her own room. But though she had supposed, for the last few hours, that what she wanted more than anything else was the luxury of a nice private weep, as soon as she found herself free to indulge in this, tears deserted her.

She sat for a while on the side of her bed, thinking back over the conversations with Geoffrey and his father. And then, because it was not in her nature to mope idly, she got up with a sigh and unpacked the parcel of work she had brought from Huntingford Grange the previous day.

She had picked up her needle and thread and already made a beginning before the fact was suddenly borne in on her, with quite terrible significance, that she was resuming work on Sara's trousseau, which would be needed after all—because she would be marrying Geoffrey. And at this point Beverley really did cry.

The next day she went off to work as usual, outwardly composed but inwardly full of trepidation. It was not possible to guess how quickly Geoffrey might have moved, or whether any echo of the new situation had yet reached the Waynes—or, at least, Sara.

But, whenever this did happen, it seemed inevitable that there would have to be further explanations and excuses and pretence of being happy when one was perfectly miserable. And Beverley felt singularly ill-equipped to deal with any such crises at the moment.

Strange to say, however, nothing at all disturbing happened, either that day or the following one. Beverley continued to work in her room at the top of the house, and no one came near her except the maid who brought her lunch, and Mrs. Wayne who came up to ask her something about a dress she was making for Toni.

It was on the Wednesday that the crisis broke. And it was Sara herself, who with rare decision and courage, gave the first sign of it. Almost as soon as Beverley had arrived, she came running upstairs and into the room, her cheeks flushed and her eyes sparkling, in a way that made her breathtakingly beautiful.

"Oh, Beverley——" she closed the door and leant against it——"don't hate me, will you?——No, of course you won't, because you're so fantastically and wonderfully generous. Oh, I'm so happy—and you're the last person I should say that to! Please forgive me—I don't know what I'm saying—only——" she came over suddenly and put her arms round Beverley and kissed her—"you've made it all so wonderfully, unbelievably easy. And you could have spoiled everything. Most girls would have."

"Oh, no! Not most girls. Only some girls," Beverley protested. But she kissed Sara back again, because it was impossible not to when she was so transparently happy and grateful. "It was so perfectly obvious that it was you Geoffrey wanted. I'd have been an idiot, as well as a beast, to try to hold on to him."

"But the way you did it all! Smoothing everything with his father. Geoffrey told me about it."

"Oh, well—if one's doing anything at all, one may as well do it properly." Beverley smiled, with a half-amused indulgence which surprised herself.

She supposed it was spiritless of her to feel so kindly towards her rival, and to go on reassuring her in this way. And yet, for the first time since Sunday, she felt an odd warmth at her chilled heart. A sort of satisfaction over the righting of some cardinal error with which she had been living for years.

"They *had* to come together—Geoffrey and this lovely girl," she thought suddenly. "They are meant for each other. She looks a different person, now she knows she is to marry him. And he——" She recalled, almost without pain this time, the shining relief and wonder on Geoffrey's face when he had realized that he was free to marry Sara.

"It's all right, Sara," she said slowly. "I'm glad we all found out in time. It would have been so perfectly awful if all this had happened *after* I had—had married Geoffrey."

"You're an amazing girl," declared Sara, with a

smiling little shake of her head. "You manage to speak so—so objectively and with no ill feeling——"

"I *have* no ill feeling!" Beverley exclaimed sincerely. "This was something none of us could have foreseen or prevented."

"But don't you—" Sara hesitated—"I suppose I shouldn't ask this, and yet I want so much to be reassured—don't you feel angry and miserable that such a thing should have happened to you? Or is there perhaps—Geoffrey hinted there might be—someone else, with you too?"

Beverley wondered just how closely this dangerous pretence was going to cling to her. But, with Sara looking so eager and anxious, there was only one reply to make.

"I can't say much about it yet, Sara, but—yes, there might be. Anyway, please don't spoil your own happiness with any worry about me. Things have a way of working themselves out—and I don't think this situation is going to be any exception."

"Oh, Beverley, you darling!" Sara—who had never shown herself half so demonstrative before—hugged Beverley again. "I can really be happy now, without a bad conscience. Everything is simply wonderful!"

And, radiant with fresh happiness, Sara went off, presumably to tell either her family or Geoffrey that everything was indeed all right.

Beverley wished now that she had detained Sara long enough to hear just what had happened—how much her parents knew, if they approved and so on. But it was obvious that, in her new-found happiness, Sara cared only about the one salient fact that she was to marry Geoffrey, after all. Everything else was a matter of irrelevant detail.

Later, Mrs. Wayne came up, with some sign of embarrassment in her usually self-possessed manner. But all she said was,

"Miss Farman, I'm sure you don't want to discuss this new development with any of us. But I hope you don't feel too badly about Sara's engagement. I mean her new engagement." She coloured slightly and bit her lip.

"No, of course not." Beverley wondered how many more people she was going to have to reassure, in this synthetically bright way. "Geoffrey and I made a mistake. We both recognized the fact. And—and I hope Sara and he will be very happy."

"Thank you." Mrs. Wayne hesitated again. Then she went on determinedly. "Do you still feel willing to go on working for us?"

It was Beverley who hesitated that time. For she saw herself, in her mind's eye, stitching away at Sara's wedding-dress. But she could not afford to quarrel with her bread and butter, for a matter of sentiment, she told herself. And so she replied quite calmly,

"I don't at all mind continuing to work for you, Mrs. Wayne. But I don't feel that it would be very—suitable for me to make Sara's actual wedding-dress."

"No, of course not," Mrs. Wayne agreed very willingly. And then she went away, with the air of a woman whose problems were working out better than she had dared to hope.

For the rest of the day Beverley worked on without interruption, until, late in the afternoon, the sound of footsteps galloping up the stairs intimated that Toni was home from school and on her way up to the sewing-room.

She burst in, breathless and evidently full of news and drama, and her first words were,

"Oh, Miss Farman—I *was* right about Sara and Geoffrey Revian, all those weeks ago, wasn't I?"

"Yes." Beverley smiled slightly. "It seems that you were."

"It's all settled. Did you know? She's going to marry Geoffrey."

"Yes, I know."

Toni drew near.

"It all happened so suddenly, didn't it? Have you heard about it?"

"Not in detail. But you can tell me—if it isn't private."

"Oh, it isn't *private*. The whole family knows," Toni declared. "It seems Geoffrey rang Sara up yesterday and asked her to meet him in the afternoon, and she found he wasn't engaged to you, after all, and so she got engaged to him herself, and then they came back here in the early evening—it would be just after you'd gone, I think—and they told us all."

"I see. How did your parents take it?"

"Oh, the usual way parents do, you know," said Toni tolerantly. "They were a bit taken aback at first, but quite pleased afterwards, because, even if Geoffrey isn't such a good match as Franklin, he's pretty good now he and his father are friends. And they'd been so upset about Sara *not* marrying Franklin, that I suppose they were quite relieved and delighted that at least she was going to marry Geoffrey."

"I suppose they were," agreed Béverley a trifle dryly.

"Anyway, Geoffrey said his father wanted to see Sara—" Beverley had a sudden desire to laugh nervously at the familiarity of that—"and so he took her back to his home with him. And I went too."

"You went too?" Beverley looked astonished. "How on earth did you manage that?"

"I asked," Toni said simply. "Several times. And, after a while, Geoffrey, who was in a wonderfully good mood and ready to do anything for anyone, said, 'Why don't we take her? The old man will like her, and it might help things.' "

"I suppose it well might." Beverley looked at the little girl before her with some amusement and appreciation. "I imagine you got on very well with him."

"Oh, yes, I did," agreed Toni, with no false modesty. "And afterwards, when Geoffrey and Sara went downstairs together, to talk to each other the way people do when they've just got engaged, I stayed with old Mr. Revian and we had a nice long talk. And that, Miss Farman," she added, dropping her voice confidentially, "was when he told me about you and Franklin. And I'm *so* glad. Otherwise I'd have been quite miserable about your not having anyone, now that Sara has Geoffrey."

172

"About—about me and Franklin?" repeated Beverley, with the odd sensation that someone had slipped a piece of ice down her spine. "What did he tell you about me—and Franklin?"

"About your getting engaged too," explained Toni comprehensively. "And he said——"

"But we're not!" cried Beverley, in great agitation.

"Oh, not absolutely officially. I do understand that, Miss Farman. It would be almost too much of a good thing, if you and Sara just changed round like that. But I told him how worried I was about you. Because I like you, Miss Farman." Toni beamed at her affectionately. "And he said I needn't cry about you——"

"Did you cry about me?" asked Beverley, touched, even in the midst of her anxiety.

"Just a bit, you know. But he said I needn't, and that he'd tell me a secret. And so he did, and then I knew it was all going to be all right. And I'm so glad."

"Th-thank you," said Beverley helplessly. "It's very sweet of you to be so concerned about me. But you do understand, don't you, that this is *absolutely* private for the moment. You mustn't mention a word of it to anyone. Not to *anyone.*"

"Oh, yes. I do understand that," Toni agreed solemnly. And as though to add weight to her assertion, she licked her forefinger and drew it significantly across her throat. "I wouldn't breath a word of it to anyone in the family."

"Nor anyone outside the family, either," cried Beverley, prickling with apprehension.

"No, of course not. The only person I mentioned it to was Franklin himself, because he gave me a lift home from school. But it was all right mentioning it to him, wasn't it, Miss Farman?—because of course he knows all about it, doesn't he?"

CHAPTER TWELVE

"YOU told—Franklin?"

Beverley stared back at Toni in such glassy horror that the little girl blenched slightly.

"Well, I didn't exactly tell him, Miss Farman, because he knew already, didn't he? I just told him I was very glad to hear he was going to marry you, as soon as all the fuss about Sara and Geoffrey had died down. But that wasn't *telling* him anything, because he knew alr——"

"But he didn't," said Beverley helplessly, unable to let Toni repeat yet again that Franklin knew all about it.

"Didn't what?" enquired Toni, looking puzzled. "Didn't know about marrying you? But he must have. Because if he asked you——"

"But he didn't," said Beverley again.

"I don't understand." Toni stared at her.

"No. How should you?—It's all right. You couldn't know. But—oh, dear, what am I to do?" And Beverley put her face in her hands for a moment.

"Oh, Miss Farman, aren't you feeling well?" asked Toni anxiously. "Do you feel sick or something?"

"A little," said Beverley, who did. "But it will pass. Don't worry, Toni. And don't say a word more about this to anyone. Not anyone, *please*."

"I wouldn't think of it," Toni assured her with dignity. "I only said it to Franklin because——"

"Yes, I know," interrupted Beverley, suppressing a desire to scream. "But you spoke a trifle too soon, Toni. Don't even *think* about it any more. Except—" she suppressed a violent shiver—"just tell me what he said in reply."

"'Well,' he said, 'Who told you that?' And I said, 'Mr. Revian did, only he said it was a secret because he had only just heard it from you and——' Oh, Miss Farman, you really do look ill! Would you like some smelling salts or something?"

"No, thank you," replied Beverley distractedly. "But I think I must go and catch my bus now." And with shaking fingers she began to put her work together.

"You're sure you're all right?"

"Yes, thank you—I'm all right."

"You wouldn't like some tea or anything?"

"No, thank you," said Beverley, who felt she would never want to eat or drink again. "I just want to make sure that I catch the bus."

"You've plenty of time," Toni assured her. But she obligingly helped to clear the sewing table and tidy the room. "And I won't say a word to anyone," she added, as she bade Beverley goodnight.

Her piquant face beamed with such evident friendliness and good intention that it was impossible to say anything nasty about shutting the stable door after the horse had gone. Instead, Beverley managed to smile, in a rather wan way, and say, "That's a good girl."

Then she made her escape at last, and found herself walking down the lane to the bus-stop in such a state of agitation that she actually talked aloud to herself as she went.

"What am I to do?—What must he think?—I can't even pretend that Mr. Revian made a mistake, for Toni said *I* told him the news. I must have been mad ever to invent that story!—I can't ever look him in the face again. He must think me so—so cheap, so presumptuous. Oh, this is much worse than losing Geoffrey—much!"

Some sense of proportion forced her to remind herself that this could hardly be the case, since only pride was involved on this occasion, whereas in the loss of Geoffrey her deepest feelings were involved. But somehow the argument lacked weight.

"I must have lost Franklin's good opinion of me for ever and ever," she thought, with a despair which was worse than anything she had felt in the deepest depression of the Geoffrey episode. "He'll never think of me again as 'his' little girl in the blue and white dress, grown-up. He *liked* to think about me before. I know he did. He liked to meet me unexpectedly and to talk to me about things, and to watch my reactions. And now he'll never be able to think about me again without embarrassment and annoyance. He may even sell my picture——"

And at this thought, she actually wept a little, standing still there in the lane, sniffing childishly and wiping her eyes, while a small, inquisitive squirrel flicked his tail and watched her from a nearby tree.

After a minute or two she went on slowly again, trying to tell herself that the situation was not really quite so desperate as she had at first supposed.

"I must just find the courage to explain to him," she thought. "After all, he is about the most understanding person I know." Her heart warmed a little at the thought of Franklin's powers of understanding. "I'll explain exactly how it really happened. He'll recognize the truth when he hears it. He's so straightforward and fine himself that he knows when one is being honest. And he's so generous that he will make allowances for my nervousness when I was speaking to Mr. Revian."

This cataloguing of Franklin's good points served to raise her spirits considerably, and all the way home in the bus she thought hard about how gay and kind and generous Franklin Lowell was, because this made her feel just a little less awful about the explanations which she felt she must make to him.

"When next I see him——" she began to herself. But at once the sober reflection came to her that she simply could not leave this business to the hazard of a chance meeting. She must seek him out, to apologize and explain, before time confirmed the unpleasant impression which Toni's disclosure must have made.

"I ought to go this very evening," she thought, and her heart gave an uncomfortable downward lurch. "I ought really to have taken the bus in the other direction, right away, and gone to Elthorpe Hall. But Mother would have wondered why I was late. Perhaps tomorrow——"

But she found that the idea of putting off the evil day involved more misery than relief. And, as she walked the short distance from the bus to her home, her thoughts were still in great confusion.

They sorted themselves out with frightening clarity, however, when Aunt Ellen greeted her with,

"You've just missed Franklin Lowell. He was here less than an hour ago."

"W-was he?" Beverley looked aghast, so that Aunt Ellen stared at her and said,

"Well, there's nothing very terrible about that, surely. He does come here sometimes, doesn't he?"

"Yes, I know. B-but why did he come today?"

"To see how your mother is, I suppose. He brought her some flowers and fruit, anyway."

"He didn't come for—for any other reason?"

"Well, he did say he thought he might find you here. He seemed surprised when I told him that you were still working at Huntingford Grange. So I suppose he's heard Something."

"I suppose so," agreed Beverley lamely, and she went in to see her mother.

"Hello, darling." Her mother looked up and smiled. "You've just missed Franklin Lowell. And he specially wanted to see you."

"Did he?" Beverley moistened her dry lips. "Why?"

"I don't know, exactly. But he seemed disappointed you were not here. He stayed and talked for a while, however. He really *is* a nice fellow."

"Yes," said Beverley sadly. "Nearly the nicest person I've ever known."

Her mother regarded her consideringly.

"Why does that thought depress you, darling? It's usually very exhilarating to reflect on the niceness of one's friends."

Beverley swallowed.

"Not if you've done something that makes you think you might lose them," she burst out. Then she sat down on the end of the bed and, taking out her handkerchief, blew her nose rather unnecessarily.

Again her mother regarded her in silence, while Beverley thought, "*That* was a stupid thing to say. It sounds as though we have quarrelled, and now Mother will want to ask all about it."

But her mother did not ask anything about a quarrel. Instead, she asked in a deceptively mild tone,

"Are you in love with Franklin Lowell, Beverley?"

"In *love* with him? In love with Franklin? Why, Mother, what are you thinking of? You can't be in love with two people at once. And I'm—I mean, I was—I am—in love with Geoffrey. That's clear enough, surely?"

"It didn't sound a bit clear, the way you put it," her mother replied, still in that mild tone. "And, though I think it was very brave of you, I couldn't help noticing that you didn't shed a tear over losing Geoffrey, whereas you're crying now about a quarrel with Franklin."

"I'm not—crying," said Beverley in a choked sort of voice. "And I haven't quarrelled with him."

"Then what," asked Mrs. Farman, not unnaturally, "is all the fuss about?"

"Oh, Mother, it's the most dreadful misunderstanding!" Beverley buried her face in her hands. "I wouldn't have lost his good opinion for the world. Not for the whole world! But something so stupid and inexplicable has happened and it's my own fault, only how could I know?"

Mrs. Farman made no attempt to disentangle this incoherent outburst. She merely stroked Beverley's hair with one of her poor, misshapen hands and said,

"I don't think Franklin would make it difficult, if one wanted to explain something."

"No—nor do I—he's such a darling. But now I've missed him, and I'll have to wait, and all the time he's thinking badly of me——"

"He didn't give that impression," her mother said consolingly.

"Oh, he wouldn't to you. He wouldn't want to make you unhappy. But I *wish* I could have seen him."

"He said he was going straight home," remarked her mother, with apparent irrelevance.

"Did he?" Beverley glanced at her watch. "But I've missed the six-o'clock bus and there isn't another one until eight. And even then I'd have to walk nearly twenty minutes from the stop."

"You could have Barton the taxi," said Mrs. Farman, proposing this unnecessary extravagance without hesitation.

"Oh, Mother—I suppose I could." A gleam of relief began to show in Beverley's face. "It's ridiculously extravagant, when I could go quite easily by bus tomorrow, but——"

"Sometimes extravagance is not only justified, it's called for," declared her mother firmly. At which Beverley actually managed to laugh faintly.

"You know—I think I'll do it." She got up, looking suddenly eager.

"You had better have something to eat before you go."

"No, no. I couldn't eat anything until this is settled," Beverley declared. And her mother had the good sense not to press the point. Though Aunt Ellen exclaimed in disapproval and astonishment when presented with the fact that Beverley was going out again without having her evening meal.

"How long will you be?" she wanted to know.

"I couldn't say," replied Beverley. Then she gave her mother a nervously eager hug and kiss, and went off, leaving Aunt Ellen staring after her, divided almost equally between astonishment and offence.

By the most extraordinary good fortune, Barton the taxi was free, and when he heard he was to drive Beverley up to Elthorpe Hall, he bristled with interest.

"You get about, don't you?" he said, by which he meant that she visited outside her social sphere in a way that he found both intriguing and questionable.

"Yes," said Beverley, and that was all.

On the long drive she was forced to make agreeable conversation. Otherwise Barton the taxi would have set his lively imagination to work and decided either that she was "getting above her boots," now that she visited "the gentry," or else that there was some special and deeply significant reason for her journey to Elthorpe Hall.

179

Beverley was exceedingly anxious not to give either of these impressions, so she talked almost incessantly about the weather and the scenery and the general state of the country. And as Barton the taxi was quite sure that he could run the country a great deal better than "They" did, if only he had the chance, this topic served them well for most of the way.

As they neared Elthorpe Hall, Beverley felt her heart begin to thump and her breath to come quickly and unevenly. In one moment of panic, she wondered why ever she had committed herself to this undertaking. Would it not have been far simpler and wiser to ignore the whole thing?—to leave Franklin to suppose for himself that the ridiculous story was no more than another piece of highly coloured invention on Toni's part?

In making an issue of it like this, and insisting on explaining herself, was she not giving a clumsy significance to the story which could only increase, rather than diminish, the general embarrassment?

At this point she very nearly asked Barton the taxi to turn round and drive back home again. Only the thought of his astonished curiosity—and his consequent speculation—kept her from doing so. And a few minutes later, they drove up to the front of Elthorpe Hall.

"Will you want me to wait?" enquired Barton.

"Oh, yes, please!"

"How long?"

"I don't know." (How long did it take to talk oneself out of a hateful and ridiculous predicament?) "Perhaps half an hour. I—I'll come out and tell you."

"All right with me," Barton assured her, and, taking out his evening paper, he prepared to give earnest study to the ways in which "They" had been mismanaging the country during the day.

With slightly faltering steps Beverley approached the front door and pulled the big brass bell-pull at the side. Almost immediately a severe-looking maid opened the door, and to her Beverley made her timid request.

"Please—is Mr. Lowell in?—and can I see him?"

"I'll enquire, madam. Will you come in?" The maid

stood aside and admitted her to the hall which she had last seen in company with Franklin himself and Sara Wayne.

"Who shall I say, madam?"

"Miss Farman," said Beverley, and swallowed nervously, as she wondered what effect—embarrassing or irritating—the announcement of this name would have upon him.

The maid went away and Beverley, too nervous to sit down, stood there waiting.

But in a matter of moments she heard footsteps returning, and it was Franklin himself, not the maid, who came to fetch her.

"Why, Beverley—what a pleasant coincidence! I wanted to see you today. I actually called in at your place——"

"Yes, I know. I've just come from there. I heard you had been. That's why I came." She spoke rather jerkily.

"But how quickly you've come."

"Yes. I—I got Barton the taxi to bring me. You see, I—I guessed why you wanted to see me, and I had to come and explain because——"

"Well, why don't we go into my study?" he interrupted, with a slight smile. "We don't need to stand and discuss things in the hall. Can I give you anything to eat?—or drink? You must have come on almost immediately from work."

"No, no, thank you. It's all right. I don't need anything," she assured him. "I just—wanted to explain ——" She wished she could get away from that self-conscious assertion, but the words seemed to come without her own volition.

"Come along, then." He ushered her into the room she remembered as his study, and set a comfortable chair for her. She sank into it, because her knees felt unsteady, and only then did she realize that there was one profound difference in the furnishing of the room since she had last been there. The beautiful portrait of Sara had disappeared, and in its place hung the picture of herself in the blue and white dress.

"Why—why, you've changed the picture. I mean—you didn't have that in here before."

"No." His glance followed hers. "I had the picture of Sara before. But, in the circumstances, I felt *she* should have that picture. I find my little girl in the blue and white dress very good company."

He turned and smiled across at Beverley, but her answering smile was rather tremulous, partly because of her nervousness and partly because she was deeply moved to find that he could still speak of the picture in these almost affectionate terms.

There was a slight pause, while Beverley found a great wordless gap where the active part of her mind should have been.

"I—I hardly know where to begin," she stammered at last.

"No? Well, then, shall I begin?" he said carelessly. "It started with Madeleine telephoning to me this morning——"

"Madeleine?" gasped Beverley, in the utmost dismay, for it seemed to her that there was no limit to the way this unhappy business was spreading. "What on earth did Madeline know about it?"

"Well——" he looked slightly puzzled—"she seemed to think it concerned her primarily."

"*Madeleine* did?" Beverley passed a bewildered hand over her forehead. "I don't understand."

"But she said you would explain everything. She asked if I had had any opportunity of talking to you recently, and if she herself had been mentioned. And when I said we hadn't discussed her in any way, she urged me to see you as soon as possible, as you had something important to ask me."

"Oh!" Sudden comprehension began to dawn on Beverley. "Was *that* why you called in to see me at home?"

"Yes. I was near, and I thought I would take the opportunity——"

"But——" Beverley had the greatest difficulty in not bursting into hysterical laughter—"I thought—oh, never mind. Let's settle this business of Madeleine first. She really is the most engagingly egotistical creature! It's about that offer you made to her, to provide her with an experimental year at the Academy of Dramatic Art. She wanted desperately to know if—if the breaking of Sara's engagement would mean you'd withdraw the offer."

"No. Of course not. But—" he looked at her curiously—"why were *you* to ask me about it? Why couldn't she ask me herself?"

"Well, she thought—she thought——" Beverley broke off, in the profoundest embarrassment, for she saw that Franklin must inevitably be linking this up with the odd story Toni had told him. "Please don't think it was my idea," she cried, almost wringing her hands in her distress. "Madeleine felt embarrassed——"

"Madeleine did? Oh, no, Madeleine never felt embarrassed about anything," he interjected, with good-humoured irony.

"Well, then, she felt it would be impossible for her to find the right moment to ask you how you—you felt about the whole thing. She—she had the idea that you were rather friendly with—with my mother and me ——"

"The perfectly right idea, I might say."

"—And she asked me to—to find a tactful moment when I could ask you whether you were going to withdraw that offer. I didn't really want to take on the task, but it seemed unkind to refuse. And—that's all," she finished lamely.

"Well—that's satisfactorily settled, anyway," he observed. "So there's no need to go on looking so distressed. You have carried out the commission; I assure you that Madeleine need have no fears about my not standing by my bargain, and tomorrow you can tell her so. Is everything all right now?"

If only she could say it was! If only she could take this cowardly line of retreat, and vow that concern for Madeleine was the sole reason for her coming to Elthorpe Hall!

But, quite apart from the difficulty of explaining her earlier confusion if she said that, Beverley knew she

183

could never go all the way back home without doing anything at all about that dreadful blunder of Toni's.

Restlessly she got up and walked to the window and back again.

"No," she declared, with dogged resolution, "everything isn't all right. There's something else——" She came to a halt in front of the picture of herself as a little girl, and before the level, friendly gaze of the child that she had been, she felt her agitation oddly less.

"When did you have this moved in here, Franklin?" she asked suddenly and irrelevantly.

"Half an hour ago." He got up and came and stood close behind her.

"Half an hour ago?" She turned her head and looked up at him. "But why—just then?"

"Because that," he said deliberately, "was the moment when I had a sudden flash of inspiration, and to move your picture in here was the only way of giving expression to it."

"I don't think I—understand."

"And I'm not sure—that I meant you to, just yet," he retorted, with a faint smile. "But if you look at me like that——"

"Like what?"

"Like my sweet, enquiring, loving little friend of many years," he said quietly, and, putting his arms round her from behind, he drew her back against him and kissed her cheek softly.

"Franklin!"

The most incredible, unidentifiable flood of emotions swept through her. For a moment it was like being someone else—someone to whom everything was wonderful and joyous and utterly right and lovely.

But then sharp and terrible recollection came upon her, and she knew that he was just being ridiculously, impossibly quixotic because of what Toni had said. He was living up to the rôle she had thrust upon him!

"No!" She tore herself away and turned to face him. "You're not to do that! I don't want you to pretend or——"

"Pretend?" She had never seen his face dark and

angry before, and the sight arrested her in the midst of her protests. "Who's pretending? And how dare you suggest I'd do such a thing? It may be rather sudden. Come to think of it, it's damned sudden to me too. But can't a man make a monumental discovery from one moment to the next?"

"But you didn't," she said very quietly. "You're just being generous and quixotic because——"

"I'm not being anything of the sort," he interrupted almost violently, "and I refuse to have such a ridiculous rôle thrust upon me. I'm trying to tell you I love you and—oh, lord, I'm sorry—" his voice dropped abruptly from its angry key—"I'm shouting at you, and I meant to be tender and coaxing and reassuring. I don't know what's the matter with me, except that I suppose I'm nervous and——"

"Nervous? Oh, Franklin——" she gave a little laugh— "*you* don't need to be nervous."

"Yes, I do. It's taken me so horribly, ridiculously long to see what I wanted most in the world, when it was right under my nose. And now I'm terrified—yes, terrified—that I'm going to bungle things and lose everything that matters, just because I was a blind fool. Help me, Beverley—" impulsively he held out his hands to her—"don't turn away from me. Please hear me, at least, and don't accuse me of pretending."

"But—my dear—" she came slowly back and put her hands into his—"I don't really understand——"

"It's quite simple," he said, almost humbly. "I love you desperately."

"But Franklin, do you mean that you—that you thought of this before Toni spoke to you?"

"Toni? What's Toni got to do with it?"

"Oh, you know," she cried reproachfully, afraid again that he was playing a part. "She—she told you—on the way home from school today that she—she thought you were going to marry me."

"Yes, yes, of course," he agreed almost absently. "It was Toni who suddenly blazed the light on the scene. I'd almost forgotten that, in my own tremendous discovery. When she said that about my marrying you, it was like a blind man finding, all at once, that he could see. I knew that was what I wanted above anything else that life had to offer."

"But then you asked her how she knew. And she—she told you the rest. Don't you remember?"

"Not really—no. I only asked her because I had to say something, so that she couldn't see how she'd hit me between the eyes. She trotted out some nonsense about old Revian having told her, and that he'd got it from you. I didn't pay much attention because it was obviously an invention of Toni's. And, anyway, nothing else mattered beside the discovery that I loved you."

"Oh, Franklin—" she went limp against him suddenly, hardly knowing whether to laugh or cry—"didn't anything else matter—really?"

"No, of course not." He held her lightly, as though he hardly dared to do so. "What else could matter?"

"I don't know," she admitted, in sudden capitulation to the wild uprush of happiness in her heart. "I suppose you're right, my darling, and nothing else does matter—except that I love you too."

"Beverley!" He lifted her right up off the ground and kissed her over and over again on her cheeks and her lips and even her charming nose. Because lovers are really nothing like so selective about these matters as the poets would have us believe.

"Stop—let me breathe." She laughed in indescribably rapturous, breathless gaiety. "I've still got something to say—to explain."

"There's nothing that needs explaining any more," he declared. But he stopped kissing her, and just held her and looked at her as though she were indeed the most precious thing in the world.

"It's about what Toni said," Beverley insisted. "It wasn't her invention, Franklin. It was *my* invention. I *had* told Mr. Revian that you and I were probably going to be married."

"But you didn't know then."

"No. Of course not. But it was when I broke my engagement to Geoffrey, and he—the old man, I mean —turned difficult because he thought Geoffrey was

186

treating me badly. And, to smooth things over, I had to pretend that I too had changed my mind and wanted to marry someone else. And then he pressed the point and insisted on knowing who it was, and—I don't know how to apologize or explain—on the spur of the moment, I pretended it was you."

She stopped speaking, and there was silence for a moment. Then, plucking up her courage, she glanced up at Franklin, and saw that he was smiling in a contented, dreamy—an uncharitable person might have said almost fatuous—way.

"You mean," he said, with a deep sigh of satisfaction, "that I was the man who came naturally into your mind at that moment? You couldn't have said a sweeter thing, my darling."

"C-couldn't I?" stammered Beverley, wondering bewilderedly what had happened to the seemingly insurmountable problem which had accompanied her into the house. "You mean—you're not angry?—or resentful?"

"Good heavens, why should I be either? You chose me, you say. I'd have been wild if you'd chosen anyone else. But, as it was, I seemed the natural answer to your difficulty—which means that you knew me and trusted me and perhaps already loved me better than anyone else."

"Oh, Franklin—" she smiled slowly and put her hand against his cheek—"I suppose you're right. I never thought of that."

"I shall often think of it," he replied with satisfaction. "Even long after we're married."

She caught her breath at the word.

"Are we really going to be—married?"

"Well, of course. What else do you think all this scene has meant?" he enquired.

"I don't know. It's just that—" she glanced round—"it's all so different from anything I've ever known before. I feel a little—lost."

"You don't need to." And, smiling, he took her hand and led her up to the picture of the child in the blue and white dress.

"Look well at yourself, my darling," he said, "and you'll see that you are completely at home. You have lived with me for years. You know all my moods, all my faults and any good points I possess. You are my best friend and my sternest critic—for you always look gravely, though sweetly, at me if I fail to come up to expectations. In fact, the only place for you is in my home and my heart."

And, while the younger Beverley looked on in wide-eyed approval, he took the Beverley he had just won into his arms, and banished her last doubts and anxieties with a long, firm kiss.

ABOUT

Mary Burchell

author of "The Girl In The Blue Dress".

Mary Burchell is one of the world's most famous and adored authors of romantic fiction.

Her first Harlequin Romance, the delightful "Hospital Corridors", was originally published in North America in 1958 (it has been reprinted several times over the years). Since then, Harlequin has published well over 60 other Burchell romance novels.

During 1976, Harlequin will be proud to publish Mary Burchell's autobiography entitled "WE FOLLOWED OUR STARS", and to further honour this distinguished author we will re-issue a limited series of her finest works.

An exciting writer, with an adventurous appeal, who discovered her flair for writing at an early age. The true to life characters and the vivid locations come alive, as she weaves the unmistakable Mary Burchell books, which have captivated an abundant following of avid readers.

OMNIBUS (1)

Mary Burchell

containing these three exciting romances...

A HOME FOR JOY (#1330) ...
is offered so kindly, by her uncle and aunt, upon the sudden death of her father. Joy was more than grateful to them, but in the end they were to benefit as much from Joy as she had from them!

WARD OF LUCIFER (#1165) ...
tells of the struggle between Norma, who knew from the beginning what she wanted, and of Justin who used her to further his own interest. When would Justin come to the realization that Norma's happiness was the most important interest in his life!

THE BROKEN WING (#1100) ...
a touching story of Tessa Morley, crippled, and her bewitching twin Tania, who had always had everything. Would she now win the love of the temperamental Quentin Otway, to whom success seemed the only thing that really mattered.

* **Each delightful Volume in the Harlequin Omnibus Series — is yours for only — $1.95.**

Mary Burchell has long since been acclaimed as "a writer to touch your heart". Her deserved fame can be attributed to the manner in which the very talented Miss Burchell weaves deep emotion, excitement and happiness into each one of her moving stories. Here we have chosen three of her most endearing novels.

OMNIBUS (2)

Mary Burchell

offers three more unforgettable romances . . .

TAKE ME WITH YOU (#956) . . .
Dagram's home was a warm and wonderful place, large, cosy and casual. Leoni had been so happy there, until that terrible night when Lucas had told her the truth. Desperately, she returned to the orphanage seeking comfort, only to find what they both needed — the key which could set Lucas free . . .

THE HEART CANNOT FORGET (#1003) . . .
Deepdene Estate should rightfully be inherited by Antonia's cousin Giles, but for some mysterious reason he had been cast out. Whilst living there, Antonia slowly uncovers fragments of family history, and begins to understand why, but everything that she learns is directly linked with the woman whom Giles plans to marry . . .

CHOOSE WHICH YOU WILL (#1029) . . .
Fourways, a rambling old house of no particular style or architecture, near Barndale, Middleshire, England. In this isolated house, Harriet Denby became companion to Sophia Mayhew, and so began the most confusing, tormenting experience of her life, involving deceit, blackmail and the disappearance of two young people . . .

* Please Refer to last page for ordering information.

MB 1947 206